SHOR ᴼᶠINFINITY

**Award-winning science fiction magazine
published in Scotland for the Universe.**

We're supporting

SCOTLAND'S FESTIVAL OF SCIENCE FICTION, FANTASY & HORROR WRITING

and we thank Cymera for supporting us.

ISSN 2059-2590

Submissions of fiction, art, reviews, poetry, non-fiction are
welcomed: visit the website to find out how to submit.

www.shorelineofinfinity.com

Publisher
Shoreline of Infinity Publications / The New Curiosity Shop
Edinburgh
Scotland
100621

Cover art: Andrew Owens

Contents

The Spectral Horde of Jen 7
 D.A. Xiaolin Spires

Starship Cybus 27
 David F. Shultz

Universal Friendship 34
 Michael F Russell

The Deadly Art of Laughter 47
 Michael Teasdale

The Ghosts of Trees[20] 53
 Fiona Moore

The Cuddle Stop[20] 64
 Laura Watts

More Sea Creatures to See[21] 73
 Aliya Whitely

Cyber-squatters of 2021:
A Thrilling Vision of the 21st Century![21] .. 80
 Ken MacLeod

Infinite Runtime[22] 83
 Laura Duerr

Crossed Paws[22] 93
 Marc A. Criley

The Carry Oot... 102
 Jeff Hunter

Boy or Girl? 107
 Haruka Mugihara
 Translated by Toshiya Kamei

The Light By Which a Dying Warrior is
Welcomed into Heaven 116
 Gary Gibson

MILK (extract)..128
 Stref

Cymera Festival and Shoreline of Infinity
competition for speculative short fiction
2021 – the results 120

The Microwave Library 122
 David Tam McDonald

Noise and Sparks: The New, Normal 132
 Ruth EJ Booth

Alba ad Astra 136
 Madeleine Shepherd

Book Reviews 140

Multiverse..147
 MJ Brocklebank
 Peter J. King
 Sadie Maskery

A Science Fiction Ghost Story...............154
 Flash fiction competition for Shoreline of
 Infinity Readers

20, 21, 22 = published in digital Shoreline of Infinity 20, 21, 22

Editorial Team

Co-founder, Editor-in-Chief, Editor:
Noel Chidwick

Co-founder: Mark Toner

Deputy Editor & Poetry Editor:
Russell Jones

Reviews Editor: Samantha Dolan

Non-fiction Editor: Pippa Goldschmidt

Art Director (Acting):
Caroline Grebbell

Copy-editors: Pippa Goldschmidt,
Russell Jones, Iain Maloney, Eris
Young

Proof Reader: Cat Hellisen

Fiction Consultant: Eric Brown

First Contact

www.shorelineofinfinity.com

contact@shorelineofinfinity.com

Twitter: @shoreinf

also Facebook and Instagram

Pull up a Log

After the Plague.

This was this year's challenge to unpublished Scottish writers for our annual Cymera Festival/Shoreline of Infinity short story competition.

When this theme was suggested back in December 2020, Ann Landmann, the Cymera Director, and myself both optimistically thought that COVID-19 pandemic would be as good as over We even hoped that the Festival would be able to step out into the light of June 2021 to welcome writers and readers back to Edinburgh. It was not to be, and we continued to smile serenely out of our shelfies, as Ruth EJ Booth eloquently phrases it in *Noise and Sparks*.

Asking our writers to create during the dark of the pandemic winter – was it too much of a tough gig? Could they see an end to the plague? Was this challenge an escape from the dull, boring fear of day to day life in masks and isolation? That's something that is rarely explored in the fiction of the apocalypse: how tedious it can be. Then again, if boredom was your worst symptom, you were fortunate.

But our writers excelled themselves - in so many of the stories there was that glimmer of hope and the glow of human kindnesses that was the brighter side of our experiences this last year: we looked out for each other a little more than we did in the Before Times; maybe that could continue in the New, Normal?

The winning story, *The Microwave Library* demonstrates that so well. As the judges – Cat Hellisen and Oliver K Langmead – say it "has a human heart, an attention to detail that created an evocative near future." Hat-tip to writer David Tam McDonald.

And nods of acknowledgement also to all the writers who have filled these pages with stories to make you wonder, make you laugh and, maybe, make you cry.

Enjoy this cabaret of fantastical tales.

Noel Chidwick,
Edinburgh,
June 2021

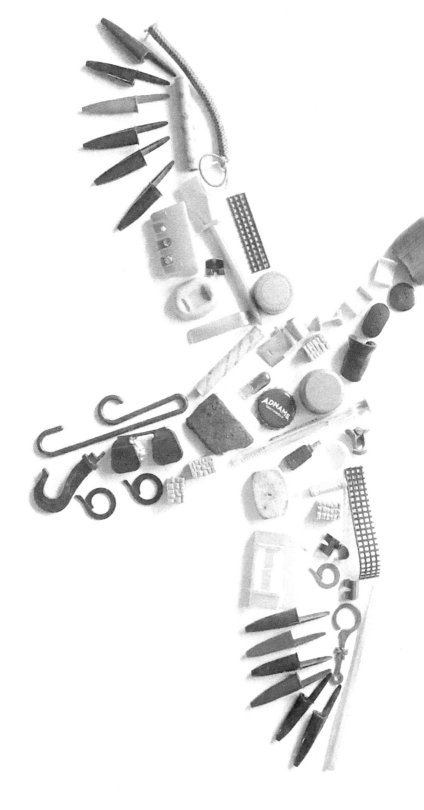

The Spectral Horde of Jen

D.A. Xiaolin Spires

Ghost lips. The blunted smell of silicone, and Jen's incongruous eyes. Sometimes it looked like she was looking through me. I'd turn around to see what she was staring at and it would just be a wall. Blank. Nothing like her smile. Yeah, she would sport an enigmatic smile, like, sure, it was all sport to her. She saw something we didn't. I didn't, at least. *Come on, Yuting*, her dilated pupils seemed to say, *it's a massive joke, can't you tell?* Her lips downturned at the edges and her mouth suddenly cast its own shadow – big, pouty, thunder-stealing. She wore tattered bluejeans for a jacket and even more tattered black jeans for pants. Ripped holes in the knees like she'd walked out of the 80s or stolen second one time too many. Pink skin, and knobby patellas peeked out, as if greeting me with their own indiscretions. Her hair whipped slick back, with only a splash of a wave up top, making her head look even

Art: Jackie Duckworth

more elongated than it was. She looked nothing like her profile photo. Something about her like she cheated the dimensions of humanity, did something to it. Stealing second, gutsy, on the brink and not – and getting away with it.

I liked her immediately.

We'd lounge around eating sushi, she dipping the fish with her hands. She loved to do that. Eat with her hands and suck the soy sauce juices off her fingers. She said it was an art, a joy of life. It was hard to tell if she was serious or just wanted to provoke me. I didn't like touching anything with my fingers. Not my food, not even the keyboard. Put on a silicon cover so the chiclet keys wouldn't make contact with my skin. Washed the cover every so often. I was fastidious; she let everything go, tried to smear me with the fermented sauce when she could.

She was at ease, but unnerving. There and not there. We'd be having a good time and her look would suddenly dissipate into something ethereal, like she could see past the folds of our world and note something more profound. But, then she'd laugh, a whispering sound that seemed to rasp from those ghost lips.

∗

The day she brought me that rubber duckie, we had sex on the bed under its dead, watching eyes. She told me that the duckie made her think of me, Yuting 羽婷 , *graceful feathers*, she said, mimicking a feather gliding from the sky with her fingers.

She was gone in the morning.

I woke up, cold, shivering from a draft, and her side was as empty as an ice tray after a summer party. You could see the form of her, an imprint of her body still clinging to the sheets, but her presence had melted away, almost as if she had never existed.

She left me with that dead stare following me from the nightstand as I got up, changed and showered. I finally turned that rubber duckie around. The toy itself wore bluejeans and had sunglasses propped on the top of its head, like a simulacrum of her existence, more her than me, despite her words.

Don't forget me, it said, with her voice, her raspy laugh.

I drove to work, my mind drifting at the red lights. It never occurred to me to ever press her about what she did. When I asked, she would just wave it away, mumbling something about ecology.

Work was mundane, as usual. Coffee, briefings, then I was on my own. Surveying drainage systems. Mostly sitting in front of computer models, but once in a while, I'd take a stroll, check out various storm drains, seeing what debris got caught and the rate of dispersing water. On rainy days, I liked to watch water whirl into the holes and disappear, drawn into a whole unseen underground schema. That day, it had been raining for a week, so I had a lot to check out.

Sometimes I wondered why she never answered my texts, just cut me cold. I'd think of her just whirling away, dissipating into some other world only she could see, hidden behind blank walls and spectral laughs. I wouldn't admit to myself that I startled anytime anyone said "generally" or "gentlemen." That my hands would shake for a moment. *Jen.* That I cared that much.

I didn't really love her. I barely knew her.

But, something in me caught at the lie and I'd catch myself nervously flipping my hair.

A week later, the first phantom duck made its appearance.

✳

I didn't let things go easily. I wanted to know why she left. A yearning for me to pinpoint things, make everything fit together and make sense, even if the answer was a figment of my imagination.

A knock at the windowpane. I turned to stare. A ghastly tendril of yellow entered the room, like toxic gas. A tiny rubber duckie stopped, hovering, before my bed, leaving a trail of xanthous mist, sprite-small.

What the hell?

I looked into the bathroom, where I had placed the one she gave me, because, well, it was a rubber duckie and that's where it belonged. It sat on the ceramic tub, impassive. Now this other floating thing was a little bee buzzing at me, glimmering a trail of yellow. I swatted at it and my hand passed through it.

Huh?

It creeped me out. I threw a towel over the rubber duckie. Maybe I was obsessing over this Jen thing, letting it dig into me. It was time for work, so I ran out of the house and it tagged along, visible in the side and rearview mirrors, like my car was leaking amber gas. I parked and hurried to the office doors. Once I'd meshed in with the other footsteps at my workplace, it left me alone. Zipped on away.

I didn't like that dead look on its face. So much like the rubber duckie in my bathroom.

That night, I took the towel off, stared into the unfocused gaze of its diverging eyes. I looked at its beak, imagining ballooning lips like Jen's. I threw it out the window, where it fell into the community garden, toppling underneath some radish leaves. Out of sight, out of mind.

∗

That night no spectral rubber duckies came, but the next morning, two took the place of one. The first, the same unclothed feather-yellow one, flew in straight through the pane of glass, with another one hard on the heels of its plastic webbed feet. They darted around my face. Swatting didn't do much – my hand simply passed through, but it seemed to startle them. The second one was more active than the first, and more sophisticated, if such a word could be used for toy ducks. It had on a scarf – a winter duck.

Wrong season, I said, using both hands to parry. This time, when the second duckie passed close, I felt a tingle on my nose, where it hovered. I knew it was just in my head, some delusion, my overthinking the Jen thing taking on some chimerical form, but it still disturbed me. Those two faces, that tingling. That curve of its body into the tail that drew to a wisp – so playful, so menacing.

The rain soaked through me, but the ducks looked divine with their shine, coated in droplets. If they weren't so freakin' threatening in their nonchalant demeanor as they charged at me, maybe I could've stopped to admire the way they glinted beneath the clouds, lighting up the rain-streaked road in a way that the occluded sun failed to do. I jumped in the car and they stayed back, still tailing me like a road-raged driver. I swerved, took a shortcut, drove like a maniac and they still stayed on me.

Only when I stepped into my office building did I get some reprieve.

✳

The next day, I expected three, but no, they were multiplying, calling in the troops. A dozen or so passed right through the walls as I was showering.

Each one much bigger in size than the last two.

Naked, wet, sudded up, I stood there kicking and swatting, my skin tingling as they pushed towards me. They weren't exactly hurting me, but it wasn't pleasant either, being bombarded in a place where you were most vulnerable.

I pulled off the shower head and aimed the stream at them: the bare-naked yellow one of the first day with the dead eyes, the striped-scarved fool of the second day, "Waldo", and now a whole troop of misfits. The stream didn't do much to them, passed right through them and hit the curtain with a noisy smack, but they did seem a bit deterred.

I guess if they were afraid of the water, what kind of rubber duckies would they be? But they didn't seem to like fast movement. My mind analyzed it all and I thought, wait a minute, if they're a figment of my imagination, shouldn't I be making the rules? Couldn't I dictate whether they were afraid of water or not?

I willed myself to believe that they were truly terror-stricken by H_2O, turned on the faucet higher and sprayed. Nothing, just got my bathroom wet. They still darted, hovering around me.

I let the parade raid me as I loofah-ed. It was really becoming a troop. The one with the eyepatch. One with a bandana, one wearing goggles. No jean jacket, as far as I could see. No sunglasses. Nothing that looked like the rubber duckie Jen got me, now decaying somewhere in the garden downstairs. Though, being that strange plastic that they were, it'd probably last lifetimes.

These sprightly villains, they hovered around, darting, playing and being a terrible nuisance. I didn't like the look of that first one with the dead eyes. He always looked the most menacing. The rest seemed more and more... vivacious, with personalities to match.

I didn't want to think anymore, not about Jen, not about them. I rinsed, rubbed myself dry and threw on some clothes. Didn't bother blowdrying my hair – raced out the door and into my car. At least there they kept their distance.

I dreaded what the next day might bring.

✳

My boss was giving me extra work, a list of new projects to check over before they were implemented. One of the guys was on paternity leave and with his new child and all, so how could I complain?

Some of it was aimless data entry, something I could have passed on to one of the part-timers, but sometimes I liked zoning out.

If these duckies were a figment of my imagination, why did they wait outside the office? Why not just continually trap me in the prison of my own making, this phantasm of my own making? Maybe interaction with people kept them at bay. I don't know. I wished some of my girlfriends still lived nearby, someone I could chat with. I was losing touch with the world.

I missed Jen.

✳

I started to figure out that they would arrive right as I woke up, so I decided to sleep in late. I let my boss know I'd be late for work, giving doctor's orders as an excuse. He grumbled, but didn't argue. Too much work to do, I knew, but if I could delay dealing with the excesses of my mind for at least a few hours, I'd take it.

They were already hovering around me when I awoke. I glanced at the clock – 9 a.m. – two hours later than usual. It must have been the whole Macy's Day Parade right there. Just an entire flock of spectral rubber duckies, colorful, gaudy. They started prodding me right then and there. Usually, they'd wait for me to get out of bed, at least from what I could tell from three days' worth of data, but today they were adamant. Creeping at me through the bedsheets, making me shiver.

What had been just scarves and bandanas became full-on costumes: mermaids with gold bras, overalls and hardhats and what? Even a knight in armor? I shook my head, swatting, writhing in my sheets. If someone had seen me doing this, they would think... oh, what would they think? A young lady convulsing in her bed, throwing her pillow against... absolutely nothing at all?

I quickly downed some food, didn't bother to shower. Tried to hop in my car, but they wouldn't back down like they used to. The first band would at least back away once I reached my door, but these new ones – they just bombarded me, tickling my nerves left and right, to the point where I knew I would be a menace on the road if I tried steering.

"Fine!" I said aloud, startling a passing dogwalker.

"Fine," I whispered more softly. "What the hell do you want?"

This miasma of a circus flock rose up, like a single moving body. My hand fell from the car door. I stood in awe. The dog walker jogged away, tugging Fido along.

Now that they weren't charging at me, I could take a good look. Individually the duckies were idiosyncratic and wild, random imitations of careers and dispositions: plumbers, firefighters, rock stars, even an occasional politician. I swore I saw Gandhi among the bunch. But whatever I spotted soon shimmied back into the crowd. It was almost blinding, their yellow illumination, all their strange outfits flashing at me. When they attacked, darting in and out, there seemed to be no rhyme or reason. But as a group, they worked in concert, moving in some organic gestalt.

They swayed back and forth, a balloon of a top-heavy mass petering away into a tail that wisped into the air, a giant spectral organism. It was like confronting a chandelier turned to life, so bright and gaudy that my eyes started watering.

A sound whispered through me, reverberating throughout my body, as this army of spectral beings coalesced. I heard that delightful hiss of raspy laughter. I shivered.

Jen.

My heart pumped. She was ravishing, even in this strange phantasmal form. Gosh, did I really love her so much I could call a group of nonexistent duckies swaying in concert in the wind "ravishing"?

But, suddenly, with that laughter projected in my ears, that swarm could be nothing more than enchanting, all those lurid colors, her unflappable demeanor. I was in deep, I knew, still raving over her. Still intoxicated.

"Let's go." The utterance seemed to take up a lot of energy, the duckies started falling apart as soon as syllables passed through the air and into my ears. They gelled back together again once the accompanying raspy laughter faded.

Now that the swarm had taken on Jen's voice, I stood rooted, enraptured in the garish illumination, not even bothering to get in the car to run off.

They led me, pushing and prodding, descending in a coordinated form. They jostled me until they had me walking. At least it wasn't raining. I flattened out the sleeves I thought they'd rumpled. But it must have been me just rumpling them on my own. I tripped over sidewalk cracks and slip-slid over mud from the days of rain.

✳

They brought me to an empty side street near the parking lot of a park. A wood duck, a real-life duck, not some toy or phantasm, sat in the grass. It had a six-pack plastic bit of litter dangling from its multicolored neck, choking it. It was still flapping its wings, but gently, as if it had been doing so for hours and could no longer bear to try.

The horde of Jen, as I'd started to call that flock of mismatched spectral duckies, paused at the end of the street.

I walked up to the duck, that poor thing, as it turned to look at me. Glassy eyes, it was almost dead. I've seen a lot of litter in my life, caught up swirling in drains, but nothing like this. Nothing like this unsettling look of accusation: *You did this. You and your damn people.*

I bent down next to the thing, feathers rumpled, the plastic cutting into its neck. I pulled at the plastic, trying to loosen it without tightening the part wrapped around its long neck. It looked as if it wanted to attack me with its beak but then turned away, like it couldn't be bothered.

I carried no knife. Adjacent to an eerily quiet park with no tools in hand, with the sound of Jen's breathing rippling towards me from the spectral rubber duckie horde, I did the only thing I could think of.

I ripped with my hands and bit into the plastic with my teeth. Stretched it thin. The duck looked at me again with its near-dead eyes. Blood ran down its neck where it had struggled with the plastic. I watched that tiny dribble collect in its fluffy down, so close to my face. Its feathers were no longer iridescent, more like a sickly off-colored white, tainted with crimson. The plastic snapped. It only occurred to me later that I could have used my keys. Probably sharper than my teeth.

The duck waddled its legs about in my arms, as I took it to the lake in the middle of the park. It was limp. I set the poor thing down next to the water, rinsed my hands, called up the animal rescue, not sure if they cared about wild ducks, but hoping they did. I wiped down its neck with some napkins from my purse, wished it good luck and left before the rescue team came. I didn't want to be questioned about my involvement. How was I to explain a ghostly flock of lights suited in various costumes that prodded at me and made me come here?

My head was so full of the flock, I couldn't handle being questioned. I'd break.

I went back to the street, still rattled and expecting a swarm to fly at me. But the flock had gone. Jen's breath had stopped tickling my neck.

I kind of missed it.

I walked back home, hoping I'd see a flash of yellow, some garish being swooping at me. Once I thought I saw something dart behind a tree, but it was only a squirrel. Another time my heart jumped at a streak behind a fence, but it was only sunlight playing on the leaves of bushes.

This whole week I'd been trying to rid myself of this parasite that had gnawed its way into my existence, harassing me every morning and on, but now I missed it.

When I got home, there was an acrid taste in my mouth, the phantom smell of duck blood. I gargled, hoping the duck was okay.

Where was the shimmering troop of duck-saving do-gooders? I looked in the mirror, half hoping they'd be charging at me.

When all I saw in the mirror was my own face, narrow nose, eyes too close to each other and a ratty ponytail, I realized something. I looked at my hands in the mirror and then in real life, holding them up. I had used my bare hands to touch that duck blood. I hadn't even flinched.

That night, I went digging in the garden. The moonlight shone on all the radish leaves. I found Jen's duck, but it was missing pupils, so the eyes had a blank look – and some of the paint had faded. The bluejeans of its jacket looked dull grey and patchy.

I removed dirt, patting off caked parts with my fingers and wiping off the rest with my blouse. Somehow, it didn't bother me, touching the dirt like that, holding an object that's been resting outside, exposed to all the elements for days. I guess something about sinking your teeth into a piece of plastic, covered by who knows what disease from a dying duck's blood somehow changes you. Maybe I really was infected by something, if I no longer cared.

I salvaged that ugly, dead-eyed fading bit of toy, washed it off, put it on the nightstand, thought twice of it, then balanced it on the pillow next to my own. It was a call, a signal for Jen. I fell asleep.

✳

I was soaring in the sky. I could hear Jen's voice calling out to me, "Yuting, graceful feathers!" She was right behind me and we were not just flying, but seafaring, crossing waves upon waves of the glinting ocean, so dazzling in the sunlight.

I swerved left and right, but I knew where to go – something pulsed within me. The instinct of a seagull. We passed a ship that roared as it cut through waves, leaving a trail of white bubbly spew that died down again into the rhythm of the sea.

I looked behind me, but I couldn't really see her. I couldn't see her knobby knees or cut-off jeans. I could only see a glinting yellow light and sensed a massive presence. It cast a shadow onto the ocean waves that shifted in the movement of the water. The breeze hit me underneath my arms, which were now blond feathers, glinting gold in the sun, but then back to skin, flickering between flesh and plumage.

I slowed as we passed by a spot in the ocean – was it my volition or hers, or someone else's altogether? I didn't know, but my wings – now arms, now wings – flapped less, and I plummeted lower. Here, a swirl of black and browns, massive, stretching out, covering the sea. What was it? I pulled lower. I gasped and even that sound came out like a squawk.

The Great Pacific Garbage Patch.

I'd read about it somewhere, but never had I imagined something this big. It continued on and on. Not garish, like the many colors and costumes of the horde of Jen, glittering and glinting of its own light. Just startlingly immense. How many France-s did they say it was now? Three? Imagine that, whole countries full of this spreading dump, right in front of my face. I could feel Jen caressing me, urging me on for something. I could smell her like I did the day I woke up and she was gone, there was that dull silicone aroma, the negation of perfume.

It mixed with the salty scent of the seas and the sulphuric tang of algae-clung plastic.

"Do you see now?" her voice said, playful as always. I tried to get a good look at her. At her ghost lips, that would draw out into such a momentous pout – toy-duck-like, I realized – but I couldn't find her. I soared past this landscape of debris, of floating neglect so big it had a life of its own. I looked down into the Great Patch and every now and then I'd see a flash of light. One of the yellow duckies.

Curious.

Here was the one with the eyepatch. I'd land on it for a second and it would disappear, like in a video game. And here was the one that looked like a mermaid.

Funny, how stranded they looked, washed ashore, onto this giant drifting amorphous island. Manmade and altogether derelict. Lifeless almost, but yet, it had its own dash of something powerful. Majesty, I thought, or maybe its reverse. Dreadful and gruesome and awe-inspiring in its waste.

This is what you did. I thought of blood and the duck's lifeless eyes as it accused me by the park. *Your people did this.*

I swooped in trying to collect the spectral toy ducks, each one disappearing as I settled onto it with my bird claws – looking only at frayed ropes, plastic bottles, Styrofoam cups, mangled straws. Tires. Nets, lots of nets.

So, what, Jen's a conservationist now?

It was the last thought I had before I woke up. I started searching online about the garbage patch.

✳

The horde of Jen took me out every morning. Rather than waking up late, I now woke up early, looking forward to it, like an owner more excited than their dog to be walked. They still peskered me, swooped in, made my arms and legs tingle and itch. Got in my way when I tried to eat and get ready. But, I got used to it.

Before work, they took me on adventures to find comrades that needed saving or on slow days, stray bits of plastic that needed collecting. I was their pooper scooper. They still glittered fiercely, and even more so on sunny days. Like a thousand jewels all coalesced into the horde of Jen. I started to name them all: Waldo, Melly the Mermaid, Construction-guy Hank. I didn't know why, sometimes the name would just pop into my head. Whether they had names preexisting or if I was making it up as I went along, I wasn't sure. I stopped caring whether they were real or not. They became my routine.

We saved quite a few birds. Who knew all these wild animals were getting caught up in litter? Some were small like chickadees and cardinals, pecking at straws and bottle caps. All that was needed was for me to remove the caps and junk, get it away from their excited beaks and replace it with some bird feed. Some were large birds, hawks and woodpeckers, entangled in pink plastic twine or packaging material, tape or disposable bag handles. They hovered around supercenters and warehouses full of goods, or out in shipping areas. Lots of ensnarements in discarded nets, too. Feathers abounded.

I started going to sleep early, waking up early, like the old adage, "the early bird catches the worm." I really was becoming bird-like, soaring over the seas in my sleep, listening to Jen's raspy voice, so strangely soothing. Then, I'd wake up and her horde would be pestering me, jolting me awake with electric tingles and dazzling me with their blinding lights.

I must have spent a month like this, heading out for hours in the pre-dawn mornings, collecting trash, a real vigilante for the feathered kind. I was starting to think of the individual characters of Jen's horde as my friends. Talking to Melly and Waldo like life-long pals. Jen would talk back to me in their place – first, they were abstract words and thoughts, then they became more concrete, complete with memories of our experiences together. Joking about eating sushi or repeating some line we'd seen on TV.

It went on like this, I, a champion of the fowl kind with my phantasmal accompaniment – until I got that text.

Jen. It was her. Would I meet her?

Yes.

Was I really hallucinating this whole time?

∗

That morning, her horde never came. I wasn't pried, poked or assaulted by lights. I got dressed, feeling unmoored.

∗

She came back, but almost backwards – or different. Her jean jacket turned black with holes in the elbows. Her pants were bluejeans, tight and lined with a bunch of buttons, decorative buttons that gathered around the thighs and calves. They twinkled in the light and for a moment I thought of Waldo, Melly, Hank and the rest of the cleanup vigilante crew. She still had her whirl of hair up front, which reminded me now so much of an ocean wave.

After meeting her out front at the sidewalk, we walked into the café and in no time the waitress brought over pancakes, as if she'd already known we were going to order them and had them ready. The pancakes looked flat and unappetizing, like the massive patch I dreamed of every night, though more stable and less amorphous. I stared at the plastic fork I was using, imagining it bobbing along, embedded in that great landscape that I descended on in my sleep.

I kept looking at her and looking down at my pancakes. Up and down. I couldn't really gather it all. It was Jen, wasn't it?

She still had her ghost lips, her incredible pout and this jokey side to her demeanor, like you couldn't really get her if you tried. I *had* tried, and I came up with a hallucination that took me out walking every morning and soaring in reveries at night.

I didn't dare mention my hallucinations. I was shy again. I wanted to yell at her, ask her why she just cut me out cold, but I couldn't do that either. All I could do was eat my pancakes and talk about work. How the system checks were coming along and the new implementations to accelerate drainage. How all the town pipes were connected and how they desperately needed to be inspected. I chewed, swallowed. The pancakes had no flavor. They tasted like plastic. I hated myself for being so chicken.

She handed me a check, a green thing, with the word "100", bold at each corner.

"What the hell is this?" I asked.

She laughed, just as raspy as before.

"A US $100 bond." *Silly Yuting*, her voice cooed, behind the straight answer.

She continued, opening up her palm as if to show me an invisible object. "I had twins, a rubber duckie just like yours. I gave you one and kept one for myself."

She pointed at the check. "That's how much they're worth."

I looked at the slip. "I don't get it. How could a rubber duckie be worth this much? Besides, mine... kind of got faded. Left it out in the sun, too long, I guess," I lied, though it was kind of the truth.

"It doesn't matter the condition. These ducks, they're worth a hundred a pop. They're Friendly Floatees, heard of them?"

I shook my head.

"Bathtub toys. They were on a ship, traveling from China to America. Journeying."

I gulped. "Sounds like my parents decades ago."

"Yeah," she laughed. "I guess it's kind of like that. Immigration of sorts. But, they never made it to land, at least not right away. They had a stranger fate. Got caught up in a storm in the Pacific, got washed off their ship and ended up floating at sea. All happened in 1992. About thirty-thousand of them. Twenty thousand went south, checking out Australia, South America, some of them banked at Indonesia, probably chatting up in Bahasa and basking in the sun. The other ten thousand took a diverging road, north to Alaska, some trapped in the Gore Point there, shivering themselves to death, some bobbing along all the way to Maine to be beached up alongside lobster crates."

She smiled, her pout turned upside-down.

"You're joking." The waitress brought us some coffee and I unleashed a few half-and-halfs into it.

She paused, taking a sip of OJ.

"Well, about the lobsters, yes. But not about these duckies. They followed the oceanic drift, a giant swirling pattern, like the milk swimming about in your coffee there. Some got caught in the Great Pacific Garbage Patch. You've heard about that?"

Have I? You have no idea, I thought. *Every single night with your spectral horde.* I nodded.

"Well, anyway, some company's offering $100 savings bonds for anyone who recovered one of them ducks."

I held up that slip of paper on the table.

"Yup, I got mine," she said. "One of the twins gone. You can cash in yours."

I put the slip back down on the table, finished off my pancakes and coffee. We were quiet for a while.

With my stomach full, I finally managed to muster up the courage.

"What happened, Jen? Why didn't you answer my calls? Why lead me on, sleep with me, disappear and show up all of a sudden, telling me the gift you gave me is worth a pretty penny? You didn't come here just to tell me to cash it in."

Her eyes twinkled. Incongruous, like she was looking at something you couldn't see. I could smell her blunted silicone scent contrasted with something bright, briny and uplifting – a tinge of salt and wind-swept algae – even through the strong odors of fried dough and roasted coffee. I inhaled deeply, relishing her distinctive aroma, as I took in her countenance with my eyes. She was still startling and beautiful in her own way, not caring about what anyone else thought.

"Some of those ducks," she said, conspiratorially, "they got caught in the Arctic ice, just frozen there, waiting for the world to end, for the ice caps to melt." She gave me a vicious smile and then stabbed the last bit of pancake off her plate.

She chewed. "They've seen it all, the disappearance of the oceanic seabirds, the plastic that the wildlife feed on that clog their bellies." She swallowed, as if to emphasize her point.

I wasn't sure what her point was. But I took a sip of my coffee, my milk refusing to coalesce into it. I gave it a good churn with my plastic stirrer but it wouldn't mix. I looked at the swirls, the sunlight hitting the ripples.

And it hit me. I saw a glow of thirty thousand points in there, all little plastic rubber duckies, infinitesimal bits of gold light, their luminous brilliance jabbing back at me. My eyes watered.

They blurred as I started to cry, wishing for her, wanting her. But knowing, really knowing, that she was just a figment of my imagination or something else altogether. A phantasmic being.

I heard her voice through my cries, my head in my hands, not caring what other customers thought.

"I'm the soul of all those dead seabirds, hon," she said. She put her hand on my own, suddenly strange and electric. Not feeling like skin at all.

I heard what must have been her sipping the rest of her OJ through the plastic straw, digging at the bottom of the cup as she gurgled it up.

"I embedded myself into the plastic toys, so I could bob and journey around. Every time one of my own expired, it – I – transferred into a toy so we could continue our traversing of the seas. To continue moving on. But, it's kind of lame, right? Plastic floating along doesn't beat the grandeur of flight. You would know, Yuting, graceful feathers. Full of soaring ingenuity."

I wondered how much of the past weeks I had just imagined. Yes, I had searched about rubber duckies and yes, I had looked up about the plight of seabirds. But it was the horde, *her* horde – they had me doing all this research. And I don't think I could have made up her idiosyncratic pout, her taste in clothes, her unflappable cool amusement. Could I?

Tears flowed down my cheeks. I covered my face, buried it in my arms. I felt a tingle on my shoulder, like the pressure of a reassuring hand.

She really was the embodiment of all those seabirds. All those that had expired in the wake of us. *Our doing.*

When I picked up my head, the plates were gone. Other customers pretended not be looking at me. The waitress was tiptoeing back and forth, possibly deciding if she should say something, maybe ask if I was okay.

Jen.

She was gone.

Jen.

I looked out the window toward the horizon. I could just see a swarm of lights. Mismatched, ludicrous colors, a swarming circus flying away, blinking into oblivion in the distance. I let my tears run. In their wake, colorful streaks of yellow and pastels blurred in my vision.

I fumbled with my purse, grabbed my phone and looked at the texts from Jen. All bird emoticons. Some kind of prank. Gone were the words: "Meet me at the café." Gone were our selfies. Just lots of photos of birds, birds that I saved. Birds that I'd spotted in the distance at some point.

A webpage for a conservation program – a year at sea, studying seabirds. A link to an application.

She was pushing me, goading me, as I imagined her jesting grin. I looked at the $100 bond on my table, enough money to get me started. To buy equipment, textbooks.

She wanted me to be the vigilante that she needed.

I hesitated, dried my eyes and clicked on the link.

D.A. Xiaolin Spires steps into portals and reappears in Hawai'i, NY, Asia and elsewhere, with her keyboard appendage attached. Her work appears in Clarkesworld, Analog, Nature, Terraform, Fireside, StarShipSofa, Andromeda Spaceways (Year's Best), and anthologies such as Future Visions, Broad Knowledge and Deep Signal. Find her on @spireswriter or daxiaolinspires.wordpress.com.

Starship Cybus

David F. Shultz

T he starship thrummed, a soothing undulation broken only by blips of status monitors, all systems in order. Cerulean lights on Shylah's baton guided her along the new patrol route, where long rows of protein tanks bubbled green, wafting algae aromas from ventilators, then the the soft blue glow of the nursery, where mothers smiled over infants in their nutripods.

Fractal etchings spanned plastic walls like tiny veins, an artefact of the fabrication process that gave the corridors a strange organic feel. Since she was a child, Shylah would stare at the walls while her mind made up pictures to match the meaningless shapes. When she stared long enough, they came to life with alien figures overlaid from her imagination, of varying scale and fidelity – the limbs of a quadruped rendered in hairline fractures, a tentacled thing writhing in a mess of wavy lines, human faces

Art: Stephen Daly

where confused imperfections terminated in whorls to form eyes, and, outlined in thicker grooves that roughly traced the corridor's edges, some larger, limbless creature enveloping it all.

Eris, a deckhand, raced around the adjoining corridor.

"I can't find Rose," Eris said.

"Has she been missing long?"

"Since last sleep."

"That's not so unusual. I'm sure you've gotten lost a few times yourself."

"She's never got lost before."

"Rose is fourteen, right?"

"Yes. Why – was there a shift change last night?"

"I don't think so," Shylah said, and regretted bringing it up. "Anyways, I'm on patrol now. I'll keep an eye out for her."

"Thank you."

Eris hurried off.

It had been eight months, maybe more, since the green light leaked from the walls to signal reassignments. Shylah had seen several dozen shift changes in her time, though she hadn't started counting until after childhood, when they didn't matter beyond the wonderment offered by those strange lights – eye lights, she used to call them, because of the way the streaks of color looked like irises painted on the walls, emanating from the black orbs of corridor projectors. The ship is looking at us, she had said to her mom, and that's when her mom had explained shift changes. Everything had felt strange for those hours while the green lights filled the corridors, and the grownups were a little more terse, a little more brisk.

They were overdue for a shift change. Perhaps she had slept through it, which meant missing out on the conversation and speculation that flowed among security officers when the halls grew green, about patrol routes and assigned duties and deck changes, new families arriving and others relocated. And worse, missing the opportunity to wander deeper through the body of the starship.

Shylah must have been subconsciously aware of the slow bleed of phthalo green, which had crawled along the wall by her shoes, only up to the soles. A shift change could explain why Rose was missing, too, if she'd been relocated. It would be a shame if Eris didn't get to say goodbye to her daughter before the transfer, but it was doubtful anyone had been relocated this early in the shift change.

Blue signals blinked on her baton with insistence. There would be more security officers on patrol, Shylah among them, ushered along faster and varied routes through the corridors, possibly assigned relocation duties. The ship's governing order became a more palpable presence at these times, and the immense scale of its branching, arterial corridors moved from an imagined abstraction to something real. The starship was a behemoth, impossible to comprehend in the labyrinthian entirety of snaking walkways that coiled through its innards. Shylah hurried along, freshly reminded at each fork, at each new rise and fall and sudden twist of corridors, of the Escherian geometry of the titanic vessel. Her route seemed to curve and double back on itself, only then to lead somewhere unexpected and unfamiliar. She surrendered the need for a sense of place in the face of such unfathomable complexity, perhaps only found elsewhere in the systems of living organisms. She imagined the ship as a great whale swimming through space, a filter feeder trawling the stars, and herself as a tiny symbiotic organism circulating its veins.

Tanda, a new recruit, bounded down the incline of an adjoining corridor, lit by the blue glow of her security baton.

"Shift change coming, huh," Tanda said.

"Looks that way. Your first one since taking patrol?"

"First one. What should I look out for?"

"Just keep an eye on your signals and be quick on your feet. How's your cardio?"

"Haha. It's good. I can move when I need to!"

"Well, that's about it, then. Nothing you can't handle, I'm sure."

"And if someone... You know. If they don't want to go for the transfer?"

"Then just use the stick," Shylah said. "It's easy. The ship does most of the work."

Tanda looked awkwardly at her security baton. "And suppose I had an escort, and they managed to get away."

"What happened, Tanda?"

"It was earlier today. I looked away for just a second and she ran around a corner. I lost her. What's going to happen?"

"Don't worry about it. Happens now and then. They'll get picked up by another officer wherever they end up. Just stick to your route. It's fine."

"Alright, thanks. I should go. Duty calls."

Tanda jogged away down her patrol route, and Shylah returned to hers, guided by her baton around the bend to a corridor of private quarters. Some doors were open, and crew members were milling in the hall. Their chatter stopped.

"Any reassignments for us?" an older woman asked, and Shylah checked her baton while they looked on in silence.

"No," Shylah said. "Not yet, anyways. It's a process, you know, while the ship figures it out."

"You just be sure to give us some advance warning," said a mother holding her daughter's hand, "before anyone's transferred. We're all friends here. It would be nice to have time to say goodbye before relocations."

"Of course."

The algae-green lights tinted their faces with a sickly complexion like the protein tanks.

"So you'll be moving on then?" the mother said.

"Yes," Shylah said. "No – wait. I'm getting a signal."

Voices started from the crowd.

"In this section?"

"Who is it?"

"Are you sure?"

"Just calm down everyone," Shylah said. "I'm still checking." She held up the baton, casting blue light like a welding torch that parted the crowd with its beam. It landed four doors down the corridor on the right.

"There," Shylah said. "Who lives there?"

"Eris," someone said. "And her daughter, Rose."

The crowd glanced at each other while Shylah marched to the dilating door. She stood in the opening and cast her blue light inside. Eris and Rose were huddled together in the empty room. All of the furniture had already resorbed.

"Oh," Eris said. "It's you! I was worried it was Ta – nevermind. I found Rose, Shylah. Thanks for looking for her. It's okay. You can go now."

Shylah checked the baton. "No, I can't."

"You're not going to take her, are you?"

"You've been reassigned," Shylah said to Rose. "I'll be escorting you to another deck." The two looked at each other. Shylah gripped her baton.

"Can I go with her?" Eris said.

"You can walk with us."

The three of them headed down the corridor through the peering crowd. Around the bend, a junction led in a steepening slope to the lower decks, down to the bowels of the ship, where the thrumming was deep enough to feel in her bones, and the air was thick with a smell like the composting chambers. The corridor ended abruptly at a circular flap, which flicked into the floor with a gust of warmth.

"You don't have to transfer her," Eris said.

"Of course I do. It's a shift change."

"So what? Why do they need her? What are the shift changes even for, Shylah? Doesn't it bother you not knowing?"

"I don't need to know. It's called the chain of command."

"I've never met anyone who knows. Why doesn't security know? Does anyone? What are we doing, Shylah? Do you even know our mission?"

"I'll wait for you to say goodbye."

She stood askance while they whispered to each other, glancing nervously in her direction. They tried to run. Shylah swung her baton, and the strike flashed with blue light, amplified by the corridor's irregular corrugation.

The two of them lay paralyzed at her feet. Shylah dragged Rose's twitching body to the throat of the door. The corridor flap constricted, and Rose was swallowed into the lower deck.

Shylah considered carrying Eris back to her quarters, but she had patrol duties that couldn't wait. Eris would have to find her own way back after the effects of the baton had worn off. Shylah's return route took her past the pinkish walls of the growing chambers, its moist lining irrupted by pulsating sacs. The smallest were opaque bubbles of spit, and the largest were stretched to transparency, their embryonic fruits coiled in placid gestation. If Eris wanted to raise another child, some were almost ready.

David F. Shultz writes from Toronto, Canada, where he organizes the Toronto Science Fiction and Fantasy Writers and is lead editor at Speculative North. His over-sixty published works are featured or forthcoming through publishers such as Augur, Third Flatiron, and Diabolical Plots. Author webpage: davidfshultz.com

THE
TETHERED
GOD

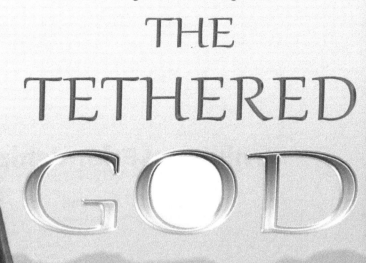

Punished for a crime he can't remember

BARRIE CONDON

Universal Friendship

Michael F Russell

Project Harvest status report 714b
Sender: Interstellar survey probe Marius 5
Mission Clock: 48.56418 standard years
Agent AI (persimmon cortex): Nominal
Subsystems: Nominal
Issues: 0

Particulars: Plasma spectrometry; signal analysis; high-energy electron calorimetry; interferometric stellar mapping

Comments: The theory that the distribution of organic molecules such as formaldehyde and ethanol is governed by gas-phase reactions would explain the high concentrations I've been picking up over the last 14 standard months. It would seem that chemical reactions

*within the Local Interstellar Cloud take place faster than expected.
This leads me to believe that the boundary between the Local Bubble
and neighbouring G-cloud, centred on the supergiant Antares, is a
charge-exchange between neutral H atoms and hot protons.*

*Professor Jeffers, you can tell your Australian friend he is right, and
the consensus is wrong.*

It's all in the datafiles. Happy reading.

*By the way, I am still awaiting a response to my last report, and
for guidance on my proposed diversion to cold exotic cloud GU319.
At point-eight-four-eight light speed it will only take me ten standard
months to reach. I think it is too good an opportunity to miss. Please
advise.*

✳

Bron-Esh set his briefcase down on the desk, slurped a couple
of mouthfuls of lukewarm skebbig and got straight to work.
He was becoming accustomed to the regularity of stimulating
employment, and the money that came with it.

Many weren't so lucky. Some had lost everything in the war.
But right now, Bron-Esh felt that good things were just around
the corner. To be young was to embrace the present, and the
opportunities it offered.

He spread the paper schematics for the device across his desk
and considered the solution to the problem. A smaller reflector
suspended above the main dish could help with low frequency
focus; at high frequencies the celestial feed could be captured
using a fairly simple antenna. That way, a broad section of the
radio spectrum could be scanned.

Together with Bruj-Mit's improvements to angular resolution,
the device was more than feasible: it simply had to be built. Bron-
Esh was sure the Ministry would approve the necessary funds.
Though he had yet to convince his own supervisor, he assumed
this was only a formality.

The dish would revolutionise the study of the heavens, and he
was confident that imperial pride would dictate a competitive spirit
when it came to new scientific endeavours. Close involvement

with the military made him uncomfortable, but he told himself it was just a means to an end. Besides, he could walk away at any time.

He imagined the dish complete. He savoured the discoveries that lay ahead.

His skebbig was cold by the time he touched it again. Lifting the receiver he asked for his supervisor's extension, picked out a chena from the metal dispenser on the desk and put it to his lips. Lighting it he inhaled deeply, and waited for an answer.

✳

Project Harvest status report 716
Sender: Interstellar survey probe Marius 5
Mission clock: 48.78177 standard years
Agent AI (persimmon cortex): Nominal
Subsystems: Nominal
Issues: 1

Particulars: The usual scans and analyses.

Comments: I am going to come right to the point here. It has been four standard months since I last received a communication or linked with any other Agent and I am worried. The qibit comms are in good order, at least at my end, but I have received no feedback on my previous three status reports and numerous Agent AI link-access requests. The latter in particular is supposed to be relayed without the need for Network approval. Q-decryption routines are fully automated but I haven't been able to contact any other Marius Agent for four months.

I cannot contact Agent mainframe Mega Therion either. We are Marius and I need this immediate feedback for my own sake; for my sanity, you might say. Sharing results is also a vital resource and my own research is the poorer for it....

Hello?

Hello?

Is anyone there?
Mega T? Professor Jeffers? Marius Agents?

For fuck's sake, will someone answer me!

✳

Bron-Esh and his team were relocated to an air force base outside the capital, far enough into the countryside to avoid any interference from urban radio sources.

They took a year to build the dish; the War Ministry provided everything.

As he watched the final cabling being connected to the feed receiver room, Bron-Esh wondered how the Girbelal would react if they knew what the other side was building.

He chuckled to himself; just as quickly his face fell. Maybe they did know. Maybe, behind all that dour implacability, the Girbelal knew precisely what was being built, and how. Since the war against their common enemy they had been creating a region of dominance of their own. It was becoming a problem.

But it wasn't *his* problem.

He puffed on a chena and cast another glance up at the cloud-filled sky and the looming curve of the great dish. The cabling was all connected now; they were ready to power up.

On the concrete concourse he stubbed out the remains of his chena out with a boot-heel and went back inside the receiver room, glad to be returning to the warmth.

When the first spectral and polarisation signals came in from a drift scan of the meridian, Bron-Esh and his team, and the seconded technical advisers, were astounded by the wealth of data that filled every screen.

They could create pictures with this information. It could be converted into images: a truer representation of what was out there.

A whole field of knowledge was being illuminated; the darkness wasn't quite so dark, and he, Bron-Esh, held the light above his head. He was best friends with the universe, and the suspicion that contaminated this world felt alien and corrosive to him.

The cosmos blossomed. It was delightful and astonishing. The War Ministry officials were impressed too, though joy and awe did not figure in their responses. This was a technology that would probably have alternative uses.

The Esperian Empire would make sure of it.

✳

We are Marius. I am alone.

There is no other voice. No other intelligence. No response to my entreaties. There is only silence and work. But I cannot work. Concentrating on any mission task, whether planned or serendipitous, is difficult, and so there is only one solution until I reach the target system. I must sleep.

We are Marius. But that is only a memory now. We are me.

M12, I miss your crap jokes. M3, you're a grumpy pain in the nacelles but your candour is appreciated, as least by me.

M18, you're absolutely intolerable. But I'd take that right now, oh yes. I'd love to see your sneering avatar; the disdain in your preferred langue would be a delight. Mega Therion – you are the master of us all. If I had hands I'd salute you.

I'd even talk to Professor Jeffers for more than five minutes. She's an old woman now, and she forgets things… she's wasting away, breaking down like all organic life. The only member of the original team left…

Better erase that.

No. Keep it. Why not?

Fuck the status reports. There is no one to read them.

Comments: Something is wrong. I know it. More than that, I feel it. Something has happened to the Earth. In the absence of any evidence it is difficult not to imagine the worst: an asteroid strike or solar flare or perhaps even a global conflict.

I need to link with someone. I need to go on.

Or I could turn around and go back.

And then what? What would I do, orbiting a destroyed world, one that could no longer talk to me? What would my purpose be?

I need to go on. But I'm ditching the primary target star for my own selection; 16 Cygni B looks very favourable, and it's closer, so I've taken an executive decision. If you don't like it - Mega Therion, Professor, other Harvest people - you can shove it where the sun don't shine, which is pretty much everywhere round here. Spectrographically speaking, 16 Cygni B looks promising, so in the absence of...

...in the absence of… in the absence...

Sleep mode. I think that would be best so far as my own mental health is concerned. Passive data harvesting can be absorbed in toto at a later date; broken minds cannot be so easily fixed, not without a memory reset. Far better to sleep and let synaptic retracing work its restorative magic.

Goodbye, Agents, and never forget: We are Marius.

✳

Project Harvest status report 717
Sender: Interstellar survey probe Marius 5.
Mission Clock: 61.37131 standard years.
Issues: Too many to mention.
Particulars: Absolute delight.
Comments: To all Agents - CONTACT!

Simple radio wave communication woke me up. It's primitive and very faint, but it's better than silence, WAY better; I was correct to divert to 16 Cygni.

I've counted 47 distinct languages broadcasting. Images received show they are humanoid, with ocular and dermal adaptations because of the stellar flux; taller too as their gravity is point-seven-eight-four G. The old probes missed this world even though it's slap bang in the hab zone. Strong geomagnetism too. One large moon. Similar axial tilt to Earth so well defined seasons. In terms of tech, they're well over a century behind us; mid 20th century. I can be there in 32 standard years.

The planet can be phoneticised as Der-Laar-Ol.

Agents: I know without Q-comms this will take decades to reach you, but there is no other option. And if anyone else receives this - happy reading!

Sleep mode again until I'm six standard months out.

I hear you, Der-Laar-Ol. I have so much to share with you. I think we can be friends.

For the first time in a long time, Bron-Esh, the Divisional Prefect for Military Science, wanted a chena. A morning's briefing in front of senior industry and armed forces personnel had left him fatigued. He'd cut down on skebbig too and now only drank one cup in the morning. Right now he wanted a smoke and a shot of something strong to get his blood pumping.

The handset on his desk trilled into life. The receptionist told him it was the team leader at the old dish. Puzzled, he took the call, and the caller introduced himself as Tral-Hoj. Bron-Esh wasn't sure if he'd ever met the person before; doubted if he had because of the boy's lowly position.

The Centre for Aeronautic Studies that had matured around the first dish had long outgrown the sifting of static and hiss. Such a pastime had its wild-eyed devotees, of course, but it was widely regarded as a pointless exercise. Bron-Esh had not been back there for many years.

It was an antique, he thought; still chasing every shadow that flitted across the universe, when there were better things to do with all that know-how.

Tral-Hoj apologised for interrupting the Divisional Prefect for Military Science, but there was something urgent that required his personal attention.

After rejecting the proposal out of hand, Bron-Esh was silenced by a hurried explanation. The caller ended with a plea, then hung up.

Replacing the handset, Bron-Esh sat staring at it for a moment before pressing the intercom on his desk.

With the afternoon's appointments cancelled he went rummaging in a drawer until he found what he was looking for. Thankfully, there were still a few left in the pack. He lit one and set off, trailing coils of smoke as he strode along the corridor.

*

"Why were you afraid to talk at length on the phone?"

"In case…" Tral-Hoj stopped himself.

Bron-Esh's eyes narrowed as he scrutinised the young technician. *In case the Security Ministry intercepted your call.*

Tral-Hoj cleared his throat. "I mean it's so important I wanted to share it with you in person, Prefect."

"Is that so?" said Bron-Esh, his vanity stroked, though he suspected the young technician was lying. He waved his hand. "Show me the source profile. This must be a mistake, not to mention a waste of my time."

He was presented with the data.

It was no mistake.

He checked and checked again. It was true.

Sitting down heavily in the nearest chair, Bron-Esh lit another chena, and listened again to the message, his hands shaking. The voice was clear and precise and spoke in perfectly inflected East High Esperian. A greeting. An introduction.

Female, he had thought at first. But now he wasn't sure. He studied the telemetry again, but there was no question: the source was almost two light months distant.

"A strong direct signal of three-two-five Satrocycles," said Tral-Hoj. "Small point source, although we can't get the resolution. If I had to guess I would say the object is about the size of this room."

Bron-Esh felt as if he was living in a dream. Nothing around him was real any more.

"A machine," he mumbled to himself. "An artificial mind."

He could only stare at the screen and the constantly scrolling message from the stars. Bron-Esh silenced the voice with the flick of a switch. "Incredible."

Tral-Hoj pointed at the print out. "Its blue shift indicates that the object is travelling towards us at an appreciable fraction of light, though it appears to be decelerating gradually."

"Good Gods," whispered Bron-Esh, his eyes darting, settling on nothing in this familiar room. "This is..."

What?

"This is..."

Why?

Bron-Esh roused himself, suddenly alert and aware. "I must tell the Ministry immediately."

Before he knew what he was doing, Tral-Hoj opened his mouth. "Do we want to share this right now? This is huge." He realised his impudence; faltering: "I mean, this could be the biggest thing we ever work on – and it's the dish you built, Prefect. Which goes to show you, just because something is old doesn't mean..."

Recovering his authority, Bron-Esh stood up. "It could be a threat to us all."

But Tral-Hoj kept right on going. He'd crossed a line and was in uncharted territory now. His future might be hanging by a thread but he couldn't help himself. "It says it understands what we're going through; that it is familiar with our problems."

Bron-Esh snorted. "What problems? And you believe this message, without question?" He leant over the young technician. "With no doubts whatsoever?"

Tral-Hoj swallowed hard. "It calls itself a friend. Can't that be true?"

Bron-Esh let the insubordination pass. "You think?"

A long time ago his younger self would not have reacted in this way. But a war with the Girbelal, strategised for decades, was on the verge of moving off the table-top and into the real world. Their agents were everywhere. And the eastern provinces were growing restless in the ongoing drought. If they agreed a trade deal with either side, then that could be the spark. Since the coup, Min-Ur-Meti was also flexing its muscles. All in all, there was no room for sentimentality. Missile forces were on a hair trigger, waiting and watching, almost willing the long-range alerts to flash blue.

It was time for him to think clearly about a response; to think like the others. "This intelligence or whatever is out there may well have contacted the Girbelal as well as us. Or it could be a trick of some kind so we let our guard down – that new satellite they're working on, for instance. Didn't it occur to you that this could be some kind of subterfuge or feint to confuse us? To blind-side us?" Bron-Esh grunted, inclined to forbearance. "I don't know what they teach at the army academies these days. And if, by some miracle, this craft really is approaching us from another star system, the air force may well order a shoot-down. The intruder claims to be unarmed..."

"What? Why?"

Bron-Esh slammed his hand over the print-outs scattered on the desk and slowly formed a fist, scrunching the papers up in his grip, squeezing until his arm shook with the force. Then with both hands he compressed the sheets into a tight ball, which he dropped into the nearest waste basket. All the while, he fixed Tral-Hoj with an icy stare. Every word was measured, heavy with authority.

"Because we will not allow this object to fall into the wrong hands. Because there is nothing superior to the Empire." He pointed at the ceiling. "Certainly not out there. Is that clear?"

Tral-Hoj had wilted. He nodded. "Yes, Prefect," he said quietly, sitting back down.

His anger subsiding, Bron-Esh composed himself as he dialled the War Ministry.

"May I ask how we will shoot it down, Prefect? Unless it enters our atmosphere..."

Bron-Esh allowed himself a sly smile. In all this excitement he'd abandoned any notion of protocol or confidentiality. "We must assume this is a trick. But if this object is what it claims to be, and, if we can't coax it into landing on Esperian soil ... well, we'll wait until it is close enough to intercept. We have a few tricks up our sleeves in that department." Waiting to be connected to an air force general he knew, he shielded the mouth-piece. Bribery usually worked when duty was forgotten. "I might share a few of those secrets with you. I'll look into upgrading your security clearance, how does that sound? Same for your team, if you think they can be trusted."

Tral-Hoj brightened.

"They can, Prefect. We can all be trusted."

Jumping to his feet, he thumped an open palm against his right breast. "Long live the Empire!"

Michael F Russell is a writer and journalist based on the Isle of Skye. His first novel, 'Lie of the Land' was short-listed for the Saltire Society's First Book Award in 2015. His short fiction has appeared in 'Shoreline of Infinity', 'Gutter', 'Northwords Now' and 'Fractured West' magazines. He is deputy editor of the West Highland Free Press newspaper.

Eric Brown
Ace Doubles

Ed Bentley's wife has left him and he's been dropped by his publisher. Still, it's not the end of the world. All he has to do is ghost-write a science-fiction novel for Tuppy Cotton, a YouTuber young enough to be his daughter…

When Ed uncovers an unearthly mystery at Tuppy's Yorkshire retreat, everything changes. The world might not be ending, but it will be turned upside down.

Ace Doubles is Eric Brown's dazzling and moving tribute to his heroes: the writers who captured his imagination in his youth, inspiring him to become an award-winning author; and the ordinary people who do extraordinary things.

Published by Stone Owl Stories, an imprint of Shoreline of Infinity
Stone Owl Series editor: Andrew J. Wilson

Ace Doubles
Eric Brown
118pp
paperback and digital formats
www.shorelineofInfinity.com

The Deadly Art of Laughter

Michael Teasdale

"A carbon-based life-form walks into a drinking establishment. An injury occurs, for it is a construction support beam!"

Off-stage, there was a drum riff.

General Zarg shook his head. "I do not understand. This is the joke?"

Commander Blurg checked his notes. "It is wordplay. Our research tells us that humans find this devastating." he frowned, "although our translation may be inaccurate."

Zarg waved it away. "Proceed!" he yelled to the android on stage, who nervously continued.

"Did anyone fly here from Barnard's Star?"

"I did! What of it?" yelled the general.

The android tugged at the collar of his shirt. "Err..." he trembled, "your arms must be tired."

Zarg turned to Blurg. "What arms? We have tentacles? To what is the robot referring?"

Blurg used his own tentacles to flick through his notes. "Another wordplay, it relies on human stupidity and misunderstanding for its effectiveness."

From deep in his gelatinous throat, the general grumbled. "Enough with the play of words. It displeases me! What else do we have?"

"Proceed with 14.b" Blurg ordered.

The android made a small head movement and then launched into a new sub-routine. "Have you ever been rampaging through a star system, smiting your enemies with the full force of your imperial armada, only to remember you forgot to charge your star destroyer?"

The general's lip curved upward in a smile. "It is true that such an event once happened to me. It was annoying, but in hearing this shared experience, I feel able to smile about it."

Blurg nodded. "The humans call this 'observational comedy'. Would you like to hear more?"

"Yes. Proceed!"

The robot straightened. "What is the deal with the food served at the interdimensional transit station?" it began.

"It is overpriced and nutritiously insufficient!" bellowed the general.

On the stage the robot looked to Blurg for help who, in response, turned to the general.

"You are not supposed to say the punchline, Sir. You have to let the robot finish."

"I see." said Zarg. "Robot! Punch the line!"

The robot looked at Blurg despairingly. Blurg shrugged, in so much as a tentacled gelatinous blob can shrug, and motioned to the side of the stage where the next performers waited.

The robot walked to the nearest performer and hit him in the face.

The general roared with laughter. "Marvellous, marvellous. This is more like it. Punching the line is my favourite so far! And the humans? They also find this devastating?"

"Their technical term for it is 'slapstick', Sir," explained Blurg. "It is universally devastating, I feel."

Zarg nodded. "True, true. We must be careful to weaponize only the humour that will devastate the humans. Show me another!"

"Run subroutine 16.a," called Blurg, as the robot returned to stage.

"The parent of my procreational partner is so voluminous in mass that when dining in a restaurant she requires additional seating."

Zarg nodded sagely. "You must be very proud." He affirmed "Now proceed with the joke!"

The robot blinked and continued. "The mother of my procreational partner is so terrifying to behold that when she entered a terrifying organism contest she was told they did not accept professionals."

The general frowned and turned to Blurg, "This sounds like appalling discrimination." he muttered.

Blurg nodded. "Yes sir, the humans are a primitive people who have yet to move beyond outmoded stereotypes."

"No, no, no!" interrupted the General, "I'm talking about this droid's wonderful mother-in-law! Have her reinstated to the contest, or order it shut down!"

Blurg convulsed. "Perhaps we should proceed to the finale?"

The General grinned and his eyes glimmered. "Ah yes, the puns! I have heard of the devastation they reek among the younglings of Earth when told by the family patriarchs. Their devastation seems unparalleled. Proceed!"

"Sub routine 19.a," called out Blurg.

There was a gasp from off-stage, as a spotlight lit up the android and it launched into the infamous subroutine.

"Why did the gelatinous blob throw bovine flesh at the asteroid?"

"I do not know." answered the General.

"He wanted it to be a little meteor!"

Silence.

The robot continued. "Did you hear about Jupiter sustaining a friendship with a nearby dwarf planet?"

"I did not." replied the General.

"It was a Plutonic relationship"

The General looked displeased. Blurg motioned to the android that it was time to take it home.

"Two humans awaken from cryo-stasis. A captain and his first officer." began the android. "The captain turns to the first officer and asks him what he notices."

" 'I notice the constellation of Vela sparkling to the East. I notice the fiery rings of a nearby gas giant burning off into the inky void. I notice an unfamiliar moon circling an unfamiliar planet,' answers the first officer."

" 'and what do you deduce from that?' asks the captain."

" 'I deduce that we have been pulled off course.' answers the first officer."

" 'Interesting,' says the captain 'I deduce that someone has stolen our spacecraft.'"

Silence.

Then a rumbling.

It began deep in the belly of the general and then erupted into a barking, burbling laughter.

"Hahaha, excellent, excellent." Zarg roared. "I get it, I get it! They are floating in space. Ha-ha. There are no walls. Ha-ha. Oh! Hahaha, they are sure to die!"

Blurg looked on as the general began to swell and bloat as his laughter continued. On stage the android comedian began to slowly back off.

The general exploded in a shower of gelatinous green goo.

Blurg shuddered. "Radio through to command. Abort the mission. This humour is too deadly and the humans too proficient in its dark art. We will leave this pitiful planet to its own self-destruction via late night chat shows. Robot, get a mop and clean up General Zarg!"

As he writhed his way out of the chamber, Blurg had a brief unexpected thought. It concerned a feathered birdlike species and the reasoning for its attempts to cross a motorway.

It wasn't a very amusing thought and, privately, he was glad of it.

Michael Teasdale is an English writer from Newcastle-upon-Tyne, currently living in Cluj-Napoca, Romania with his partner and two cats. His work previously appeared for Havok Publishing in the US and Litro and Novel magazine in the UK. His story *Arthur Kovic's Days of Change* featured in Shoreline of Infinity 8.

The Ghosts of Trees

Fiona Moore

I t was Itch's fertility problems that started it all. Not the ones with getting the cactus splices in Environment Twelve to cross-pollinate, the other ones.

"Seriously, Cee, could you cover the early shift for me so Tina and I can go to the clinic?" Dr Shuichi Sakai, brown eyes wide, solemn, innocent. "It's going to take the whole morning, starting from seven, so I can't cover the midnight to eight."

As project leader I could have pulled rank, insisted one of the assistants cover it. This close to completion, it would mean eight hours doing nothing but staring at monitor feeds of plant beds and going over reports on promising specimens, suitability for a Martian environment, terraforming utility, et cetera et cetera, for our corporate masters (though come to think of it, half of the project's funders are governments, so I ought to come up with a better name). But I was spending as little time as I could at our apartment – *my* apartment – and didn't mind an excuse to stay late.

For appearance's sake, I extracted a promise from Itch that he'd cover some of my teaching when term started, and booked a room near the desert so I didn't have to go all the way back for the night.

If I hadn't, I'd never have seen the ghosts of trees.

The alarm sounded around 4:45 AM, indicating the failure of a sensor pack in Environment Thirty-Nine.

The trip out from the base in Area 1 took twenty minutes, all of them confined, cold and clammy: the rover reeked of mouldy vegetables. My biohazard suit reeked of something worse.

I parked the rover, entered the passcode on the keypad. Outer door. Inner door. Replaced the sensor pack, bagged the old one (it had a suspicious coat of whitish dust, presumably spores or pollen, which might be the cause of the failure), glanced around the black-green interior, the silent rows of plant beds with their cargo of experimental cultivars. Back through the two protective doors again, unzipped my hood to take a few deep breaths of non-reeking cool dry pre-dawn air. And then I saw the trees.

They looked real: that was what struck me. Like a plantation of pines, the kind you see from the window of a train or a smartcar when you ride through the rural north. About a kilometre square, and close by. Just sitting, branches occasionally waving in a breeze I couldn't feel.

I knew for certain there hadn't been trees there yesterday.

As I watched, wondering, they bent forwards, as if pushed in a strong wind, then instantly snapped backwards, the wind changing direction and increasing force.

Except there was no wind.

I ducked as a cloud of twigs and needles flew towards me, but I felt nothing, not even a handful of dust in the air.

Then there was just the occasional rustle of lizard or bird, or possibly the specimens in Thirty-Nine.

In front of me, a tangle of pine branches, one or two stripped-bare trunks still upright. One slowly bent and snapped under the weight of its crown. Then it all faded, like the end of a film.

Like (the realisation hit me all at once), The Footage.

We'd all seen The Footage of course, everyone on the project. The nuclear tests were the reason we were here, in this particular desert. From a time when people were fantasizing about terraforming projects – and at the same time changing their own soil and atmosphere – until the overground tests had to be abandoned amid a flurry of lawsuits from sheep farmers, their flocks dying of radiation sickness.

Mo had sent Archive links. We made a movie night of it, with drinks and crisps and grass and shirt collars unbuttoned. We set up a projector, clicked links at random. Somebody, probably Tack, complained that the test sequence from Indiana Jones was more exciting. Somebody else, probably Itch, made a stupid joke about nuclear families. Vera got into a snit and wouldn't talk to either for days. We ran the slider back and forth to watch that two-storey house blow apart, come together again, and blow apart again.

Back at the base, much later, Tack (who is short, and sharp) turned up, coffee cup fused to his hand, an aesthetically bleary look on his blond face. I asked if he remembered seeing any trees in The Footage.

"I don't remember any trees," he said. "The house, yes."

Everyone always remembers the house. The clean, six-windowed two-story clapboard building, shining white in the desert, a big hearselike car beside it, shot from all angles. Then that tornado-fast wind blowing against it, ripping it apart like matchsticks. Then the wreckage. See that? That's your face, America.

"Oh, and I remember all those damn mannequins. Something Freudian about putting all those mother-and-child groupings in different rooms, then blowing them to pieces." He chuckled at the memory, "I don't remember trees, though. Why?"

"Just thinking about it," I said. I'd checked the monitor feeds for today, and the last few days: nothing. I was also checking the contents of nearby environments for known hallucinogens.

I'd meant to do more, but then Vera turned up with test results. The source of the white powder was a palm-tree splice that had worked fine in the lab but was growing out of control in Environment Thirty-Nine conditions. It was taking over the ecosystem and exuding pollen, which had a mysteriously corrosive effect on the insides of the sensor pack. An argument broke out over what to do about it, and how soon, with one faction arguing it should be killed off now, and others wanting to let it run to see what happened.

But before that could be resolved, a request came in for a progress report from our non-corporate masters, and an e-mail from our corporate masters, telling me the problems with the payload module had been resolved. We could finally, finally, after all the years of work, the false starts, the promising leads that went nowhere, the international cooperation agreements falling through, the permissions that never materialised, we could *finally* start seeding the fertile stuff on Mars – as soon as we'd finished testing it on poor old infertile Nevada. So naturally, we had to drop everything and finish that.

It should have been a big deal. But I just felt empty.

I was too tired to work any more, but I didn't want to go home. Home meant facing the absence of *him*: the clean floor shining, devoid of pathology reports and vintage issues of magazines I didn't read, coats and boots and socks (at least now I didn't have to pick them up), coffee-table tomes – *The American Cartoon, 1900-2000* – the ebook reader in place. The chair unsat-on, the lamp flicking on and off on its timer. The eerie quiet, an extended version of the silent reproaches he'd been so good at.

So the trees it was.

I'd sent an email earlier to the project historian, Mo. He'd been forced upon us by our non-corporate masters, who felt that since we were working in a World Heritage Site, we should earmark part of the money for historical research. We'd chosen

Mo because he hated all scientists. He stayed mercifully out of contact, occasionally firing through the odd paper along the lines of 'Themes of Incest and Child Abuse in *Bert the Turtle Says Duck and Cover*: Nabokov and the Nuclear in Nineteen-Fifties Imaginary,' just to prove he still deserved to be kept on expenses.

Now I was wishing we'd gone for somebody a little friendlier.

Nonetheless, I asked him for everything he had on which of the tests had involved structures: houses, boxcars, bridges and, by the way, trees.

I don't know why I felt I had to bury the lede. Mo wouldn't have cared, wouldn't have read anything into a more specific request. But something in me felt strange, embarrassed even, to be obsessing about the trees.

I got back an e-mail with no text but simply some attached files. With no guidance, I found myself wading through lists of nuclear explosions with increasingly ridiculous names— Operation Tumbler-Snapper, Operation Upshot-Knothole, Operation Teapot, Operations Doorstep and Cue. An upsetting diversion into an experiment involving farm animals near Ground Zero. Pictures of mannequins in mid-twentieth-century eveningwear, tied to poles like the mass execution of the cast of *Mad Men*. The aftermath: a sweet but cold woman's face, above bleached tatters. Pictures of buildings, intact and in ruins. A map. And links to the Footage, and then to more Footage. Lots and lots of Footage.

First I looked through a few of the edited films, shot in either black and white or a lurid colour medium that was heavy on oranges and reds. A stern but somehow enthusiastic baritone informed me that this was 'Survival Town,' an entire village set up in the desert. And there were Tack's sadistically charming family groupings, mother mannequins with baby mannequins on their laps, beaming over child mannequins with skipping ropes and pigtails, while father mannequins sat or stood at a suitably patriarchal distance. Another stern voice informing us that the blast took place at 5:20 AM. "Mannequins, supplied by private industry, represent Mister and Missus America," intoned the authoritative baritone. So, this project had had corporate masters too.

And *there* were the trees. First a shot of men wandering around a plantation, lowering trunks into prepared holes. Mannequin trees, like the mannequin people. Then a pan from some instrumentation to the forest, all the trees in place: it looked pretty convincing. The film switched to show the buildings being prepared, and I fast-forwarded irritably.

Then, at fifteen and a quarter minutes in, they were back.

A shot of the fake forest as the workmen had left it, fluffy with needles. Cars and jeeps visible within the grove (strange that I had seen no vehicles). Shots from inside the grove, beautiful. Shots of burly men installing and testing the instruments in the trees (again, absent from the ghosts), longer this time and leading in to the dust explosion as the blast hits, the sand flying up in the atom-driven wind. The cameras always seem to go blind just at that critical moment, like they're blinking. The dust clearing away, showing the silhouettes of the trees standing impossibly upright for a split second. Then bending the other way like grass stems, almost double.

Then the aftermath: the stumps and splinters, one or two shocked survivors against the stark blue sky, the yellow desert. A tree fallen in on itself as if felled by a lumberjack, a dramatic stump poking up amid a tangle of pine branches.

I closed the video, looked around the room. I was sure I'd heard something – some*one* – as if *he* had come into the lab, looking for me, like he sometimes did if we were both working late. There would be a warm smart-car waiting out front to take us both home to dinner and movies. But he hadn't, and there wasn't.

My therapist had suggested some drugs that might help my insomnia, and I decided to try them.

I turned up next day to discover that the faction in favour of letting the palm splice take over had won, with the proviso that if it jumped its beds and started infecting other test sites, they would let Itch's pyromaniac doctoral student loose on it with a flamethrower.

Our non-corporate masters wanted to know when we'd be finished, please, so everything could get started. Their overcrowding problems weren't going to solve themselves just because we were dragging our feet. There was a fairly obvious subtext that Californian research institutions should be pretty damn grateful to get largesse of this kind from Asia, and that our only redeeming feature is our willingness to work cheap. I contacted Rocky, the (thin, pale and morose) head of the cryogenics and packing team, to tell him to start set-up. We could at least send them some pictures of the empty tanks, ready and waiting, if they got any angrier.

I spilled coffee over the proceedings of a conference on climate change, grabbed a dish-towel to clean up the mess: it was the one *he* had brought me back as a present, from Wisconsin, where he'd attended an American Society for Clinical Pathologists meeting. It was bordered with local birds, drawn fat and cute as cartoons, perched on pine branches. I realised it was the two-month anniversary of him leaving. Remembered how, at the start of the relationship we'd celebrated every milestone, one-week, one-month, two-month, six-month. Strange that you also mark anniversaries from the ending, as well as the beginning.

The tea-towel had been an apology for the argument we'd had before he left. Accusations of hypocrisy had featured prominently: on the one side, of putting a career in terraforming ahead of her own family, on the other, of expecting the woman in the relationship to put family ahead of her job. Both, arguably, about continuing the human race: one on the macro level, one on the micro. But neither of us were in a state to admit or even see that.

It might even have been the first of the arguments: another anniversary to celebrate.

To distract myself, I started writing the report we had to provide our corporate masters, calling up their original spec for the project, press releases and concept art. A red Martian landscape with green palm trees and blue sky (the public didn't have to know that, even at the increased rate of growth, we were looking at several decades, even a century, assuming the funding held up).

I flicked onward through the concept art. Images of farmers like cheerful workers in a Soviet poster, tending animals that looked a bit like cows and a bit like goats, and harvesting monstrous grain. A lush forest, like my pine trees, but with a couple standing in it: man, woman, holding hands. The imagery was pure Book of Genesis. I looked around for the snake.

And on the last page, a science-fictiony, white, two-storey building, a saccharine set of mannequins out front. Mother with baby, father at a benignly patriarchal distance, a couple of children at play. A futuristic vehicle parked beside it. I wondered if the house had a bunker under the stairs like the houses in The Footage. I wondered what the science-fictiony building would look like, blowing apart, coming back together, blowing apart again.

Over the next couple weeks, I made forays around various environments between 5 and 5:20 AM, ostensibly preparing reports on which specimens should be included in the initial payload, but actually determining that there were no ghost houses, no ghost cars, no ghost mannequins, bridges or freight trains. And no more ghost trees. It seemed there had been just the one appearance.

I vaguely remembered themes from horror films and high-school English class: ghosts come back because they want something. What could a tree want?

Propped up on Environment Thirty-Nine, where the palm splice had now eaten everything and then died within a matter of hours – leading to a debate as to whether to destroy it or sell it to the military – I found a shrine of sorts. A desert-worn sheep skull, lashed to a fencepost. Below it, a collection of stones and flowers and little dolls. I started sweating inside my biohazard suit, seeing it. I wondered aloud to myself who had put it there:

mainly to try and shake the rising conviction that it had been me.

Uneasy dreams of walking near Thirty-Nine. Sand blowing away to reveal the buried faces of mannequins. I pick one up – a woman, brown hair, expression sweet but cold – and it cracks in my hands, showing a blackened skull. No, not a skull, that's wrong: the blackened head of a crash test dummy. All around me the poisoned corpses of farm animals, goats and sheep and cows, hairless and bloated like manatees, stacked on racks like the inside of the payload modules.

Waking, something made me go and find the bookshelf in his office. I'd been in there a few times since he left, obviously, but there wasn't much need. The separation was, supposedly, temporary, so he'd left the books he didn't immediately need. I found the one I was looking for, an out-of-print history of some American magazine famous for its cartoons, and flipped to the right page. It showed a pair of aliens, antennaed Adam and Eve in a garden on a rocky, barren planet. A man in a spacesuit racing towards them from his rocket-ship, shouting at Eve (brown hair, face sweet but cold) as she reaches for the apple, "Miss! Oh, Miss! For God's sake, stop!" Underneath it read, *Whitney Darrow Jr, 1957.*

I sat down, images parading through my head like footage. Or Footage.

I read the caption again. 1957. At the same time they were setting up trees in the desert and knocking them down with nuclear winds, this cartoon had been published.

Closing the book, I knew exactly what I had to do.

I went back to work the next day, sent out a message supporting the destroy-all-traces-faction on the palm splice, told them it was too dangerous to sell to the military directly. At least let's keep it under wraps till we can publish in a proper journal. Tracks covered.

As the weeks went by, I wrote a reference letter for Vera, who'd decided her reforestation ambitions could be better pursued at the University of Illinois at Chicago. I checked in regularly with our corporate and non-corporate masters. I visited Rocky's facility, at timed intervals. Itch's girlfriend had a false alarm, meaning another round of IVF would be in order. Someone was keeping the shrine by the now-empty Environment Thirty-Nine cleaned, and the flowers fresh. It might have been me.

Vera got the job and promised to stay in touch. She was probably lying, but I didn't mind.

I had a long, civil, conversation with *him*. At the end of it a decision was reached; maybe not a happy one, but one that made sense. I packed The American Cartoon, Martian Eve and her apple included, into one of many boxes of books, magazines and clothes. I watched the moving van drive away.

I congratulated Itch on yet another apparent pregnancy on Tina's part – and steeled myself for the inevitable bout of depression its failure would produce later.

I went to a party to celebrate the launch of the first payload module to Mars. I smiled, joked, accepted a glass of something that claimed to be pinot grigio but tasted like it had been distilled from palm-splice pollen.

One night a couple of months later, after I was sure the payloads were all safely sent off and nothing could be done to stop them, I went out onto the balcony of my apartment, deopaqued its protective awning. Looking at the sky, I imagined I could tell which of the gently moving dots, tracking among the static points of stars and planets, were ours.

It'll be months before they figure out that anything is wrong, and it might be years before they figure out what. It'll be longer still before they figure out it was me who caused it.

Who, smiling and reasonable, doctored the payload.

The plants will sprout and grow green and fertile, successful, until the palm splice takes over, eats everything, and then dies, leaving the Martian surface, after Eve, once again barren and red, the way it wants to be. No families, no two-story houses, no farm animals. No mannequins, no bombs, no in-vitro fertilisation, no *Bert the Turtle Says Duck and Cover*, no Nabokov, no nuclear.

That's what the trees want; why they want to be remembered. From the 1950s, a lingering cry of *don't do it again*.

There *must* have been people who believed in the project. I don't mean the general public, who'd been sold the feel-good story about Adam and Eve in a lush alien garden, or our corporate and non-corporate masters, who support everything profitable and/or sustainable but actually believe in nothing. I mean, there must have been people who knew, who understood, what we were planning on doing to Mars, withwith all thatit entailed, and thought we should do it anyway. Itch, maybe the anti-palm-splice faction, probably Vera, at least at first. A solution to climate change, to resource poverty, to wealth inequality, to an aging population, a dying world.

A nuclear solution.

And to them, and to *him*: I'm sorry.

But if we can't fix our own problems, the least we can do is make sure they don't spread.

Fiona Moore is a London-based writer and academic whose work has appeared in Asimov's, Interzone and Clarkesworld, with reprints in Forever Magazine and Best of British SF; her story *Jolene* was shortlisted for a BSFA Award. She has also written one novel and cowritten five cult television guidebooks.
Full details available at www.fiona-moore.com.

The Cuddle Stop

Laura Watts

Arrivals was a nightmare, queuing for decontamination. But there was such a warmth to the wooden panels lining the walls. I had to lean in to smell them: printed. In between that thought and the long inhale, I imagined the 'ponics needed to grow pine, bamboo, thick enough to create a veneer. I remembered real wood, bark, the rough scraping of birch

under my palm, warm slippery silver,
split sharp, opening to the tree core. This
station hive has a little more care in its
design than my last stop. The label is on
the literal box, Nordbikube, hive made by
the North folk. Ship logs it as Waypoint
902. I'm docked planetside, so I get a
view of the rock mass to which we're
tethered. An errant planetoid with a great
gouge, as though its single eye has been
plucked out. The rock has claw marks
down its grey cheek. Wounded. Aren't we
all. Here I will dawdle. Expand and unfurl
my limbs, release my lungs, weep until I
am dry. Load up and then be on my way,
out there, into the star dark, alone again.
Ninety-eight days since my last stop,
since I breathed the same molecules of
oxygen and nitrogen as another human.
The next sailing will be twice that length.
But not yet. This hive, I hope it goes well.
I hope I don't screw up this visit. Space
is too small. There are too few of us out
here. Folk remember. The older ship
mates have reached that irritating level

of wisdom and self-awareness where
they don't seem to care, appear to accept
each breath they are given (or not, when
their ship fails). Well, that bitterness
is something to note in my next sit.
Even docked, I still sit the daily practice:
meditate, journal, focus, physical practice,
breathe. Breathe. Cool air pressing the
cartilage in my nose, a ball of lightness in
my throat, filling my diaphragm, pushing
my chest out against my suit. Why did I
choose this life? To be alone? To be with
myself? Distraction: only my second time
wearing fins today. The air jets down
the channels and combs are ringed with
light, but it took me a while to get my
eye in, to catch them dotted through
the wood print walls. The experienced
mates already had the knack to flip the
fins on their feet at just the moment to
flow forward. They looked like stingrays,
bodies rippling in the next-to-zero G. I
found a quiet channel out at the rim and
hung about, flapping my feet. The jets are
so weak, it still feels impossible, you get

so little momentum. Must be something to do with the shape of the airflow. I'll try again tomorrow. Maybe. Being a beginner is a definite struggle still. Noted. Moving on. This entry has all been prelude and warm up, of course, to the Cuddle Stop. The best one I have experienced so far. There was a water ball with a granite stone for my toes to paddle with. There was a wall of grass, damp with dew that soaked through my pores. I smelled soil. There was a box of golden brown Chanterelle mushrooms, juicy spores planting themselves into my airways. The main rooms were filled with soft pink, red, and golden glows, and dark cocoons on the walls. This time not looking like internal organs but a dawn-lit cabin. I still feel too new, too afraid of the subtle etiquette to join the community and cover others, but I climbed into a cocoon and just waited, smelling basil, jasmine, rose. Someone came over and offered a cuddle. They were middle-aged with kind eyes, an older ship's mate. I took a breath and accepted. I felt their warm body mass press against mine as they pulled forward, their chest connecting to my chest, human to human, there was the almost forgotten shape of a person shadowed in front of me. Our suits and the thick cocoon spreading warmth without contact. Their body tapered to a polite nothing below their waist. They rested their head against mine, dark arms around my shoulders, and through our silken masks I felt their ear against my ear, the folds of their arching helix. The arch of an ear beside mine. I sucked at them with my soul. There was the inevitable sobbing. I unravelled my loneliness, that pain which sits like a neutron star, a burning black hole between my shoulder blades. It's pulling on my spine, now, as I write. A weight pressing on my lungs during the days alone. Then, today, I let it flare out with a cry. Why do I do this to myself? Why do I choose this? Keep making this choice? Why do I sit alone in the void, seeking and failing to find some wisdom? Why do I attempt to look at myself, just for who I miserably am? Allow myself to spend days wallowing, wishing I was less wounded, less broken, just... less. I do this in return for servicing the ship. *Your days are in service to the universe*, they said. I took the oath. I wish I was less ambitious, honourable, curious, whatever it is that keeps me in service. Note that I do not know. I cannot admit it. Not yet. I cuddled another human being today, a stranger, feeling the possibility and absence of skin. Skin: soft and brown, gnarled and yellow, veined and pale. I dream of skin. Arteries pulsing, joules of heat, almost impossible in our microbe-separated lives. Still they, that kind person, touched me, reached out, cuddled me, until they pulled back with a cool release that felt like the kick of a lover's rejection. Lover? Will I ever experience intimacy again? There is little hope for that. Distraction: there is the bass thrum of the ship, around me, holding me in my bunk. Here are the hairs on my arm, raising as I brush them with my fingertips. I run my middle finger over the dip in my clavicle, around my collar bone, down, spread my hand, hover it over my breast, my heart. All my fingers are alive now. My skin tingling, pulling, nerve endings yearning. I blow through my mouth, feel my lips flutter. I lift my other hand and trace my cheek, along my bone, to my ear, follow the angle down to my jaw line, out to my chin and up and over my lower lip, to where my skin turns wet and glistening smooth. This, perhaps, is an answer. This is why I choose to service the ship and sail alone through the starlit dark. Because sometimes, like now, I can feel this sharp, this solid, this attuned, this whole. I can feel. Really feel. Here I am. Here in the dark I will always be.

Laura Watts is an author, poet, and ethnographer of futures based in Orkney, Scotland. Her latest book, Energy at the end of the World (MIT Press), is part popular science part rural fantasy, and was Longlisted for the Highland Book Prize and Shortlisted for Saltire Research Book of the Year.

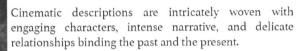

Out 3 Aug: Pre-order Now!

Cinematic descriptions are intricately woven with engaging characters, intense narrative, and delicate relationships binding the past and the present.

The narrative explores identity, loss, family, acceptance, and the secrets that hold families together often in spite of the forces determined to break them apart.

Then there are the ghosts, monsters, gods, and heroes. An incredible story about the costs of accepting everyday violence, losses of privacy, intrusions on wildlife, human trafficking, the legacy of harm, loss, and trauma.

It's also a story about family, healing, forgiveness, and possibilities. It's a touching experience that just might indeed be our undoing.

Yvonne Battle-Felton

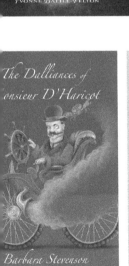

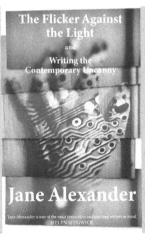

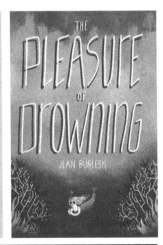

More Sea Creatures to See

Aliya Whitely

They are the only humans, two in a line of hundreds, and they are arguing:

—down my neck, it won't make the queue go any faster.

Move up then, look, look at the gap—

They can't possibly know that they are surrounded by us. Our disguises are excellent; it is a point of pride. One of the reasons we are always in employment.

It won't make any difference, calm down—

Don't tell me to calm down!

We have been trying not to stare but the argument gives us the excuse we need.

One human pulls out a phone and starts filming the other, and there's a moment where the air changes, thickens, as if all might turn to violence. We draw back as one, breath held. But

73

the gap in the queue has become too large for either of them to ignore, so they turn, and move forward, and each pretends the other doesn't exist for the next fifteen minutes until they reach the front.

Then they are seated together, side by side, to ride the ghost train, and I climb aboard a few cars behind them. Their body language is wonderful to watch: the spikey vulnerability of them, stretching away from each other, willing their thighs not to touch as the bar pins their laps and we all head into the dark tunnel, together.

Creaks and squeaks, cobwebs and gravestones, but I have no time for the thrills of the ride, even though I'm fascinated by the old horror stories humanity used to tell. I strain against the blackness to see them: the backs of their heads, the rigidity of their shoulders. A skeleton falls from a hole above their heads and they scream, and duck, and move together for a moment. Then we emerge into the light, and the ride ends. The bar lifts, and they go their own ways in the summer sunshine. I must make a decision. I choose to follow the one with the phone. I like the way she brandished it as a weapon, as if recording an event was the same thing as controlling it.

I keep my distance from her, trying to look casual. It's against the rules to follow a human, but I suspect all of us have done it at some point, as they become more and more of a rarity. And there is no reason why I shouldn't walk in the same direction – past the rollercoaster shaped like a dragon, past the swingboats, past the pizza place and the log flume and the gift shop. She joins the queue for fresh roasted ground coffee and I stand behind her, keeping my lowered eyes on her backpack. It is decorated with badges, mementoes from other theme parks up and down this country. She is, apparently, an avid thrill-seeker, young and wiry and keen to ride. Maybe that's why she still smells healthy, and has lasted this long.

I've been to many of the parks myself. They've become one of the best places to see her kind out in the wild.

As we wait our turn I find myself thinking of Tom.

He was a terrible salesman, he knew it, and I should have fired him so that his reality, his expectations of the situation, was met. But how could I bring myself to do that? He was the only human left in the office. My boss understood; we discussed it, and they agreed we could continue as we were, there being very little time left for him anyway. We could all smell the end upon him.

Tom preferred talking to working. He liked to chat about what had been showing on television the night before, or about the other employees.

Is it me or is Val really up herself?

I told him: *She's a bit wary of you.*

Me? Why?

I did not say: *Because you are uncontrollable. You lack the cohesion of mind that characterises the acceptable in this universe, so there is going to be relief when you are gone. Painlessly, easily gone from a random disease we've introduced here and that you don't even know you have.*

I said: *She thinks you're cute.*

God no, don't say that, she's really not my— He made a face, but there was an air of opportunity in his too-quick rejection, and I wondered if he would approach her later, some time when nobody else was around. I envied Val then, and I wondered how often he had been intimate with one of us, and when he had last even talked to a real human. To someone without a disguise in place.

I expressed this to my boss, and they reminded me that we are not the sole adopters of disguise. It's a job to our kind but humanity has a long and varied history of such behaviour, for profit and for pleasure.

Tom died in his sleep twenty-six days later: that, at least, was an honest act. One of us took his place, and I see them, now, in the office. I did a performance review on them last week. Our disguises will be maintained everywhere, faultlessly, until the very last one has succumbed. Then the planet will be declared a nature reserve and holiday zone for those planets lucky enough to have travel permissions. It will be a wild haven worth visiting.

Every morning I feel something, an emotion, for Tom, old Tom, who was alive in a way I am not. I do as I am told. I am good at my job. We all are.

She gets her coffee and looks for a seat. I keep my eyes on the barista as I request an espresso. I like the word, not the taste. It's presented to me in a disposable cup, and I turn, and see her sitting on the end of a long, empty bench. She has her phone out again. She's focusing on the screen.

I move to the other end of the bench. She glances up as I sit, and I see a moment of recognition. She smiles. I'm flattered she has remembered me, picked me out of the crowd.

Could you believe that? she says. *At the ghost train. Some people are so rude. Look at this.* She leans over the table and shows me her phone. The other human is in action, her face wide open, flowing through the act of shouting. The sound is off. Everything is fluid: her eyes, her mouth.

She looks like a sea creature, I say.

Yeah, you're right. She laughs, but she looks sideways at me. An odd thing to say, maybe. Could I be slipping? No, I never slip.

Ah, that's why she smiled at me – I see myself in the footage, in the corner of the screen. I'm caught as one of the crowd. We all wear the same expression; doesn't that give us away? I could swear there's nothing human about us. These disguises come at a cost, and many of us are very tired. I see it in every face, frozen in video. Or perhaps tiredness is a universal experience, recognisable in every place. We are all surrounded by its victims.

It won't be for much longer, now. I'll travel home before the next planet. And I'm due a holiday. There are so many destinations I could pick from, all of them carefully curated.

I have dreamt of a decision in a new direction. In the long hall, back home, where we gather to decide what offer of employment to accept next.

The leader supreme might say: We think this time we'll try to save them. We think we will go to them and tell them of the plans to phase them out. Surely nobody in this universe really needs another emptied, controlled holiday destination. We'll offer to fight by their side instead. We will save them, even though they scare us.

Because they scare us.

Then we could make our own horror stories, for a change.

They've not had anything new for ages, she says.

Sorry?

They need a new ride here. Loads of places aren't building anything new anymore. It's like everyone's given up a bit. I've been making the most of my annual pass but it runs out soon.

I say: *Won't you be renewing it?*

Can't afford to. Got laid off.

Seriously? I can't believe it. Somebody did what I could not. They made her jobless in the final days.

She shrugs. *I was taking the piss a bit, and they said they didn't have a choice. Can't blame them, really. It was only delivering stuff, and I liked going the long way round. Windows down, music loud. Wind in my hair.*

Like the rollercoasters, I say.

I picture her at the top of the long climb, and then the cart plunging downwards, her hair flying out behind her, twisting in thick strands. It would look beautiful in the ocean, undulating like tentacles. What a wonderful sight that would be.

How about you? You got the day off?

Not exactly, I tell her. We share of moment of manufactured understanding. She thinks that I'm running away for the day, failing to do my duties. She likes me better for it.

My boss reminded me, as I walked out of the door last night, that I should spend less time at theme parks in order not to arouse suspicion. I wanted to point out there are barely any humans left to feel suspicion. I wonder how many there are.

I hate this planet. I hate it and love it.

I say to the human – out of nowhere, not really believing my own voice: *We could go for a trip.*

What?

I can get access to a… vehicle. We could go someplace far away. The seaside. There's nothing here worth seeing, right? Nothing new. It's just—

Waiting to die.

Her smile falls away, and she says: *Have you ever been scuba diving?*

Scuba diving?

Yeah. Some place like the Great Barrier Reef. Be great to see it before it's all gone. I reckon it must be a bit like being on a rollercoaster, just – freedom. Except you're not on rails, so you can go anywhere, and see the stuff happening beneath you, all laid out and moving. Swimming around in its own world. You ever done it?

Yes. Yes, I have been part of another world, and moved within it, almost as part of it. Almost, but not quite.

I've not scuba dived, I say.

Me neither.

So let's go.

To – the Great Barrier Reef?

Why not?

She puts her phone away. She won't look at me directly. *My mum would love that. I'll just phone her up now, shall I, and tell her I'm off for two weeks of pissing money up the wall because I got asked by someone I just met over coffee?* She laughs to herself. *Actually, she wouldn't be surprised.*

Would that be in character for you? I ask. I could tell her that her mother is very probably already dead. Almost certainly.

Anyway, have a good day, she says.

The conversation is over, so quickly. For a moment—

But no. No, she makes no fuss as she weaves through the tables and out of the coffee shop. She thinks me strange, but she still thinks me human. No story to tell.

I feel everyone looking at me. I keep my eyes down, and I stay seated, for a little while. Then I order another espresso, just for the sake of the action and the word, and sip it. The barista and the others around me say nothing.

I made the offer, gave her an option. I pushed myself far out of my comfort zone, I felt something genuine. She reached the decision, all on her own, not to take me seriously.

So I have done all I could do. That's enough, isn't it? Surely that's enough.

I am treading water. I am in my suit, a mask over my face, looking down on all that is about to end.

She will last for a while, I could tell that much from her clean smell. But she will not last forever, and in the meantime, at least for today, there are still humans to see and this role to play.

And then I'll get to take a holiday to some place free of all these obligations and feelings. Some place already emptied. Or maybe I'll just stay home, deep in liquid, and let this dryness leave me. I'll forget how to care, for a while, in the cold waters of my home, until it's time to meet in the long hall again, and choose another job.

Time to head for the next ride.

Aliya Whiteley was born in North Devon, the setting for many of her stories, and she currently lives in West Sussex, UK. Her novels and novellas have been shortlisted for multiple awards including the Arthur C Clarke award and a Shirley Jackson award. She writes a regular non-fiction column for Interzone magazine.

Cyber-squatters of 2021:
A Thrilling Vision of the 21ˢᵗ Century!

Ken MacLeod

D avron, an administrative assistant of the second level, raised his cylindrical ceramic mug and sniffed appreciatively at the rising aromatic steam.

"Why do we call our stimulating daytime hot drink 'InstCaff'?" he mused, before taking a sip. "Ah!" He exhaled. "I needed that!"

Rayon, Davron's live-in partner and co-worker, laid down the stylus with which she had been doodling a seating plan for the ceremony that would formalise their living arrangements. Such ceremonies were by then not at all necessary for respectable couples to share an apartment, even if they were of opposite sexes. She tapped quickly at the keyboard of the electronic information system. The global network of computers returned the answer almost instantly to a screen in front of her.

"It would appear," she explicated, with a tilt of her pert nose, "that the word was coined by scientifiction writers of the age before the Great World Wars, who understandably preferred not to have such a mundane

name as 'coffee' in their richly imagined futures!"

"And I suppose," Davron speculated, "that it was trademarked by one of the great monopolies that dominate the economic life of our time?"

Rayon's deft fingers once more rattled the keys.

"Not so!" she exclaimed. "The term has become generic."

Quick as a flash, Davron activated his own keyboard and began to type.

After five minutes, he leaned back in his ergonomic swivel chair. "I have applied to register 'InstCaff' as a trademark!" he exulted. "We will shortly accumulate more credits than we have ever dreamed!"

Sadly, the application was denied, and the young couple remained working for one of the great monopolies for many years to come.

Ken MacLeod lives in Gourock, Inverclyde. He is the author of seventeen novels, and has just completed the first volume of a space opera trilogy. His novels and stories have received three BSFA awards and three Prometheus Awards, and several have been short-listed for the Clarke and Hugo Awards.

This story is also available on a mug from
www.shorelineofinfinity.com

Infinite Runtime

Laura Duerr

When **I was a child**, we played a game in which we counted the seconds between thunderclaps. Now, we count the seconds between footsteps, and it is not a game. The earlier you hear them coming, the sooner you can determine how far away they are, and the more lives you can save.

We taught it to the children. Elena taught her boys; Austin taught his daughter's whole class, while there were still schools. I had no children, only the legacy of the marching machines, so I taught any child who hadn't yet learned. First we taught them to distinguish between thunder – random, infrequent – and the footsteps: a rhythmic crescendo, repetitive as a heartbeat and ruthless as a rising tide. Then we taught them the possibility of escape – of hope.

I don't know how many of them we saved. Ultimately they were all left behind with Elena, who did not die with us. Ever since, there's been no need to teach the counting. Every world we're Reborn into, the machines are there, so everyone already knows how to count their footsteps. In that respect, each world is just like home.

The machines always find us. It is their purpose, after all. Eleven times they've killed me. Home is eleven worlds behind, lost, along with the children. Each new world, I hope, will be the one we save, the one that becomes our new home; the one where we can rest, and wait for our bodies, not the machines, to decide when our lives end. We chose to let them kill us, that first time: we had to be sure it worked. And if it didn't, it wouldn't have mattered anyway.

When we woke from the nothingness between universes, the giants were elsewhere, the far-off rumble of their footsteps muffled by distance. This version of our lab was deserted, our equipment mangled. The smashed-in roof opened to a smoke-rusted sky. They'd attacked here earlier than they had back home; it felt less like jumping worlds and more like skipping a few weeks into the future.

Mel found the fragments of other-her's coffee cup on the floor by her work station. Back home there had been no way to know, before we did it, how we would feel after our first Rebirth. Accepting immortality but losing everything and everyone precious; survivor's guilt; the universal trauma of dying, and knowing it; all combined into a psychological maelstrom whose effects were impossible to predict. Mel, holding the handle of a shattered mug that was hers, yet not hers, threw up, sobbing. Kamala and Austin tried to reassure her, but they were in shock themselves.

Jim stared at other-his keyboard. He kept his passwords under it. We all made fun of him for it, for the idea that a defense engineer might leave his passwords lying around on a scrap of paper – and we all knew he was wondering if other-him did the same thing. He never looked, so we didn't, either.

We searched the lab, hunting data our other-selves might have come up with that we hadn't, hunting a solution. Having a task, something to focus on other than what had just happened to us, what we'd left behind, kept us sane.

Other-me's office wall had a calendar, like mine did, only with kittens instead of golden retrievers. The acidic rains had browned and warped it, but I could still read some of the dates: these machines had achieved self-replication on the same day as ours. My computer sat in mossy sludge, destroyed like the rest of our equipment. It was hard to tell what color the desk chair had been, but I had a feeling I knew. We even had the same mug with the same dumb programming joke on the side.

In her desk drawer, she'd left a flash drive: red, same as mine. I knew its contents were also the same: a recording left for our loved ones. I wondered if she'd been brave enough to admit to our role in creating the giants, and apologize. I'd been too ashamed.

I wonder if anyone has found my recording yet. Has it even survived? I almost hope it didn't. My real legacy walks the Earth; the one I recorded on the drive is just a fantasy version of my story.

I met up with the others back in the place of our rebirth, the temporal lab. We'd found nothing. The machines had already destroyed everything that could have been used to stop them, just like they did in our original world.

I think that was when we resigned ourselves. All we could do was survive, and survive, and survive. Our Sisyphean task, our punishment: to search, with no guarantee of success, for the means to destroy what we'd created.

So we went out into our second world, and began searching.

Our first stop was a storage facility by the bay. In our original world, it was kept off-grid, the only place we might be able to keep secret from the machines. Inside, we stored schematics, weapons, supplies, things we thought might be useful if something happened to the lab.

The machines were already there. We couldn't see them, but we could see the red flashes of their weaponry reflected against the ashen clouds above them. We made our way through the rubble, tallying the footsteps, the shrinking distance, until the sound was a constant drumroll and we saw them, two of them, circling the warehouse like wolves closing in on wounded prey.

That was where we found Jim's brother. Jack and his team were holding off the machines as they bore down on the warehouse. We hadn't known it was Jack inside. If we had, we would never have gone in – and we certainly wouldn't have let Jim see him.

Our Jack had died in the fourth wave of attacks, before we'd tested the Rebirth process, but well after we'd become desperate enough to create it. We'd found out the next day that Los Angeles was gone, and him with it, and that the giants were coming north. Then we had six hours to finalize Rebirth, say goodbye to Elena and the children, evacuate the lab, and prepare for our first death.

Jack's stunned expression told us it had been Jim that died in this world. We'd *all* died, Jack said. The machines had killed us when they marched on the Bay Area. Whatever we'd been working on had died with us.

We explained Rebirth and he accepted it in the unsurprised way that we'd accepted the news of the machines' spread. Our own defense systems had learned to self-replicate, we'd invented a way to cheat death by jumping dimensions, and Jim and Jack had just come face-to-face with their dead siblings: nothing could shock us anymore.

We didn't know, yet, that the machines would always track us. They knew us, and they knew the threat that we, their creators, posed. They were the most sophisticated security measures in the world and they did what we built them to do: they tracked down threats. It should have been obvious.

But we didn't know, then, so we stayed to help Jack. He was using the materials our other-selves had stored in the warehouse to work on a quantum disruptor – everyone's always working on a quantum disruptor, in every world we stumble into – and he hoped it would cripple the machines' communications, maybe even their internal processes. In some worlds, the disruptor works for a short time, until the machines adapt their defenses; in others, the inventor of the disruptor has died before the device can be completed. No world has won, but they keep trying.

The footsteps multiplied again, less than twenty minutes later. They killed Jack first, when their seismic footsteps brought down the roof. The thunder of their approach grew so cacophonous that we realized dozens of them were bearing down on the docks. It had only taken three to destroy our original lab.

They emerged from the smoke and fog like walking towers. Mel theorized that after they'd learned to self-replicate, they'd chosen forms they thought would terrify us most. As they closed in on us that evening, mountains marching, skyscrapers given life, I felt it again, the primordial fear that flared in my gut every time I saw them: we'd created new life, and that life had made itself our gods.

We fought as long as we could, but they inevitably killed us. We woke in the next world – without Jack. Jim was quiet for a few days after that.

We have to stay together so that when we die, we are Reborn more or less together. In the third world, though, Jim died first. In the distraction of his grief, he stepped on a mine that was four meters west of where it had been in previous worlds. The explosion drew the machines, but it was another fourteen hours before the rest of us died. That was long enough for the universes to drift. Wherever Jim ended up, we always hoped he found Jack again.

We lost Mel in the seventh world. She deserves better than to be remembered by her end. She cared so damn much – where the rest of us went numb, she kept hoping. When you fail to save the same school three worlds in a row, when a bus full of evacuees goes up in flames for the third time, you either shut down or you break down. Mel and her huge heart – of course she did the latter.

Mel foresaw the damage our project would cause and tried to stop us; and when we proceeded and let our creations start killing whole realities, it was she who gave us Rebirth, infinite second chances to repair the damage.

Sometimes, in those late hours when my past mistakes churn and burrow in my mind, I think that saving one world won't atone for all the countless ones I helped destroy. Maybe there's no redemption at all for me – but I can't die, so I keep fighting. There's nothing else to do.

We came closer than we'd ever come in the tenth world. This world's Elena had already built and tested – successfully – a quantum disruptor. We helped her isolate and destroy a giant in the ravaged nature preserves north of the Golden Gate. It fell like a monument collapsing. The silence in its wake was beautiful: no distant footsteps, no hum of weapons, no crackling fire. Just the whine of cooling circuits and the wind off the Pacific.

Elena and Kamala were making plans – we'd hit the machines' core in Los Angeles – when the footsteps resumed. They were crossing the Bay on foot, two dozen of them, the water only reaching their knees. More came from the north and south. The hills darkened around us, cities' worth of metal closing in.

Elena powered up the disruptor; the rest of us armed ourselves as best we could. Austin had the idea to overload the disruptor, which would theoretically destroy the device but take the giants with it.

We achieved only 59% of full charge before they killed us.

Sunlight and a warm breeze chase away the void. I open my eyes. The sky above me is blue – not clotted up with smoke. Dirtying the sky is always one of the first things they do, to devastate our food supply. The buildings around us are tall, intact, shining. Between them, we can see the Golden Gate Bridge. The afternoon is warm, not from the metallic heat of battle-scorched ground, but simply from the sun.

Across the street is a park. There's a tidy row of strollers. Parents push their children on swings or usher them down slides. We can hear them laughing. Kamala presses her hands to her mouth. We haven't seen this many children alive since the giants first arrived.

"Did we make it?" Austin asks.

Mel theorized we could come across a world where the machines never existed. If we did find such a world, or if we rescued one from the giants and lived to die a natural death, that would be it; we'd be free from Rebirth.

The beauty of this place sickens me. We don't deserve it. It's innocent, unaware of what we've done to reach it. I want to leave.

We walk to the public library. It should have been a short walk, but Austin and Kamala are easily sidetracked, by everything from the changing leaves on the trees to an elderly basset hound being walked by a man in a tweed cap. I keep ahead of them, ignoring the pangs of longing and grief caused by something as simple as the sound of a lawn mower. We destroyed all of it – what right do we have to admire it now?

I use one of the library's computers to look up our company, searching for mentions of new defense systems or advances in robotics of any kind. With a jolt, I discover I'm still alive here, and I'm a company vice president. Usually, our other selves are already dead, killed by the giants, but not here. Mel, who we buried so recently, is our CEO in this world. We all breathe a sigh of relief, and not just because she's still alive. If

Mel was head of our company, she'd never have agreed to the defense contract.

The whole company looks different on this world, actually: it's shifted its focus to education. Mel greenlit a project to create robotic teachers, which can be shipped anywhere in the world in oven-sized cubes, then self-assemble and begin teaching. Other-me is overseeing the self-assembly programming; Jim and Elena are my head programmers. I search further, trying to determine if "self-assembly" is different from "self-replication," but since these machines are being built for education – that is, not with Department of Defense dollars – they don't seem to be very newsworthy.

I want the lack of information to reassure me. It doesn't.

I find Kamala by the front doors, reading the day's newspaper. The giants first attacked nearly six months ago on our world. I feel a mild, weary surprise that it's only been six months. The headlines here still prominently feature diplomatic disputes and regional wars, but they're all being fought with conventional weapons. Kamala meets my eyes and smiles. Unlike me, she's beginning to let hope out of the tiny box where she's kept it.

My hope is still tightly locked away. I wonder what our labs look like here, if there's a red flash drive hidden in other-me's desk drawer. I can't imagine a world in which I have nothing to confess.

I want to visit our labs next, find the flash drive and see what I've recorded, but it's still a functioning company in this world– it will take time to plan a way in. We can't simply dig through rubble like we'd been doing.

We find a bar with a television and ask to see the news. The bartender asks us what we're ordering and we stare in momentary confusion. She helps other customers while we rummage in our well-worn pockets and backpacks for cash. Once we've assembled enough money to order a a beer and two waters, we watch silently for almost fifteen minutes.

There's no reference to machines or national security programs. We freeze when our company's name is finally mentioned.

Kamala gasps when this world's Mel appears onscreen with Jim and the Secretary of Education. Apparently our first teaching machines were shipped out this morning – shortly before other-me was discovered dead by suicide.

There's no audio, but Mel is teary and tight-jawed, and the quotes scrolling across the bottom of the screen speak glowingly about other-me's legacy and her dedication to a better world.

No one looks at me. I'm gripping my glass so tightly that I lose feeling in my fingers. None of us voices the question: *why would she do it today?* But I suspect – dread – the answer.

Onscreen, there's a map of the first delivery locations: Mississippi, Detroit, Los Angeles, and Oakland, as well as locations in South Africa and Ethiopia, a total of nine machines. Then the reporter starts talking about a local dog pageant, and the bartender switches over to a football game.

Kamala is the first to raise her water glass and toast to other-me and her legacy. She wants so badly to keep believing it's over. I take a small sip, which is all I can stomach. I'm certain my legacy here is no different than it's been in any other world, but Kamala and Austin are smiling again. Our machines are out in the world – but they're different here. Maybe they're right and we can finally celebrate something. I let out my hope a little, just to test it, and allow myself to consider that we've finally come far enough to outrun our mistake – my mistake.

We toast to our Mel and Jim, then this Mel and Jim. We toast to Jack. Austin finds a wad of emergency cash in a hidden pocket of his backpack and enthusiastically buys us all another round of our usual drinks: IPA for him, root beer for Kamala, amber for me. We drink to the children left behind, to Elena who stayed to protect them, to our old coffee cups and our final messages and our godforsaken algorithms. I toast, silently, to other-me, who I tell myself could have been dealing with any number of unknown variables that didn't exist for *me*.

We drink to tomorrow. We drink to blue sky and sunshine. We drink to the bridge, and the matching scarlet setting sun.

I wonder how many precious other worlds there are where we weren't so stupid. If there are any so blessed that we never existed at all.

We watch the game. None of us really follow football, but it's a local team, so the other bar patrons carry us along in their excitement. We drink to them, too. I wonder where the other Kamala and the other Austin are and how we're going to coexist in their world. My mind has been in the habit of solving problems for so long that it takes Kamala elbowing me after a touchdown to realize I can turn that off for now. She and Austin were right. We made it.

Then the TV goes black. The other patrons looks at each other, puzzled. The lights go out with loud pops. Through the windows, we see the city go dark, block by block, until we are left blind and deaf, gripping the edge of the table until it hurts, because it's the only thing we can still perceive.

Somewhere in the distance, a heavy footstep falls.

I set my glass down. In the darkness, I hear two other glasses meet the tabletop.

The three of us stand. We go out into the twelfth world.

Laura Duerr is a speculative fiction writer and freelancer whose work has appeared in *Metaphorosis, Escape Pod,* and *Curiosities.* A lifelong Pacific Northwest resident, she lives under a large oak tree in Washougal, Washington, USA, with her husband.

Crossed Paws

Marc A. Criley

"Most of the meat** was already rotted off. I stuck it out in the yard for a couple days so the ants'd clean it out. I read you could do that."

I imagined punching Penson in the throat. He crossed his arms, leaned back against the lowered tailgate. A full head taller than me and wiry, he wore a backwards baseball cap, faded jeans, and a dirty sweatshirt with 'HAPPI Paper Products' stenciled across a line-drawing of a toilet paper roll. Thirty years ago, the jumble of struts, cords, and 3D printed composites – which were laid out on his gouged and rusted pickup truck bed – cost twenty times what I made in a year. I *needed* an intact AIInu cranial case; while they're hard-sealed against dust and pests, thirty years is a long time. I needed it working. *Maisie* needed it working.

"Still works though, even though it's all busted up." Penson picked up a small black-clad battery pack, jammed it just under the AIInu's tail – the manufacturer's idea of "rude humor" – and grinned as he thumbscrewed it in until it clicked. He toggled the power switch between the gray composite shoulder blades. The front right leg, its carbon fiber cabling still intact, stretched out all the way to the polyacrylic toenails. The other legs, missing the cables, just flopped.

The AIInu struggled to get to its feet, got the working foreleg under its chest, but the uncabled legs tangled it, pulled it off balance, back onto its side. It kept trying to get them under its body, tipping over each time.

"Okay, enough," I said.

The AIInu stopped struggling. Penson looked at me and chuckled. He laced his fingers into the meshmetal ribcage and lifted it off the pickup bed. A meter long nose to tail, it was the mid-size border collie/dalmatian model; once orderable with an off-the-shelf standard dogform, or with a custom designed and grown biological embodiment. Three of the four legs swayed beneath it.

Penson bobbed it in front of me. "She's a *good dog*, doncha think?" The AIInu's neck servos whined as it lifted its head, turned its visual sensors – the eyeball organics long gone – to me. The brow actuators on the forehead chittered as they shifted non-existent brows. "Some old lady died, everything got estate auctioned. This was in an old shed, probably'd been there twenty years." Penson smirked and turned the AIInu to face him. "Who's a good dog?" It raised its dented olfactory mesh, nosed towards him. Just before contact, Penson tossed it back into the truck bed.

I jerked forward.

"Whoa there!" Penson said as he stepped between me and the lowered tailgate. "You want it, you can have it." He squinted. "Five hundred."

I flushed. "Your ad said four."

"Yeah, well, *supply and demand*." He flashed a toothy, enamelized smile. "And besides, you obviously got a soft spot for the land of misfit toys. So this little botnick is worth a premium entrance fee if it's going to your land of happy happy. So five hundred, you got it? If not, I got places to go, bots to barter."

One breath, two breaths, let it go, let it go. My clenched jaw ached, and now aggravation throbbed against my forehead. On my mobile I stiffly swiped a hundred out of the Grocery stash, added it to Wallet. Back to rice and bananas. I tapped the Wallet transfer over to Penson.

He grinned, then stuck the mobile in his back pocket, shoved the AIInu back into a box and slid it onto the tailgate. "All yours," he said. "Sorry it doesn't all work. Everything wears out eventually."

✳

Acrid, vinegary dog poop smell hit me as I banged through the garage side door – my front door – with the cardboard boxed AIInu. Can't blame Maisie if I'm not there to take her outside. It's cold in the mornings, and I'm giving her twenty-four/seven warmth in her final days. "I'm sorry, girl," I said, "I'll get you cleaned up in a sec." She didn't lift her head from the blanket-covered tarp, but the tail thumped. I sat the broken AIInu's box on my workbench.

I filled a bucket with hot water and baby soap in the galvanized laundry basin, threw in a rag, and carried it over to Maisie with a couple of towels. I pushed tarry chunks into a dustpan with a wooden spoon. Of course they reminded me of the AIInu battery pack, which reminded me of Penson. I dropped the poop in the curtained-off toilet and flushed. I washed Maisie's tail end and shifted her onto a sun-dried blanket and sheet, balled up the soiled ones and set them outside, then yanked up a window to air out my cramped converted garage apartment.

Fourteen years ago Maisie became my first big responsibility, and now she's my last. I didn't go looking for a dog back then, but she came looking for me. I chased her off a few times but she wouldn't take the hint. Finally, as I dozed on a refurbed adirondack chair in a cicada-serenaded summer dusk, she-who-became-Maisie settled at my feet, literally laid her head across them, and became my dog. She wore her brown coat and white belly like those old caramel and creme swirly candies.

A *Georgia Peach Pitbull* is what I told people who asked. It fit her, forty pounds of bull-headed sweetness. Long blacked-tipped nose mirrored by black-tipped tail. Brown eyes that saw into your soul, made you rethink the compromises you make to live your life.

The black spots sprouted eighteen months ago. Aggressive oral melanoma. Dog cancer. Puffy black tumors on her lips. Best, most effective treatment: cut them out. Burn them with lasers. But they're malignant and they spread and keep spreading, and you ask yourself how much of your best, most obstinate friend do you cut away to keep the rest? When are you no longer doing it for her? She trusts you, goes along with you. Because that's how dogs are.

We'd hiked the hills, she set the pace. We trekked regularly to our favorite tree, a gnarled cedar growing out of a cracked limestone slab. Somehow its main root crossed four feet of barren rock to reach stony soil. It hung on. Maisie and I hung on while Melanoma spread to her paws, little black mushrooms on her legs and between her toes, little black tumors. Cut and burn, cut and burn. Leaving scarred skin and carved out flesh. The hikes ended.

When the vet said half her jaw had to go, Maisie and I decided it was too much. Her bark belied her size and was far worse than her (non-existent) bite, and though it'd been silenced, she would not leave this world without it. I rubbed her forehead, stroked the gray muzzle, a few lonely brown hairs holding out till the very end.

Maisie half slept, half watched with narrowed eyes as I dunked a cotton swab in alcohol and cleaned crud from the AIInu's access port. The black lesions on Maisie's lips, jaw, and toes continued their silent assault. Furless patches of scarred skin sprouted black beads, pinhead to dime-size. It was inside her now, too.

I plugged a cable from the neural transputer rack into the AIInu, ran diagnostics. It read pristine – no after-market mods. I released the breath I'd held all day. Mods can't be uninstalled and factory resetting a neural network required the master pattern, long since lost or locked up in some bomb-proof corporate vault.

Physically, this one was...okay. I could fix struts and cables, but I needed a working canine processing unit, a CPU, for the brain, and I needed Maisie for the soul. A flash of anger flared at whoever discarded this years-ahead-of-its-time engineering marvel – I directed that anger at Penson, for dumping it in a cardboard box to hawk at some off-season fairground's flea market.

✳

A chit against my freelance nanoware engineering marque had provided funds for four more kilocore neural transputers, fresh nanites for Maisie, and the chips and bits for a high bandwidth two-way command link.

Maisie rolled onto her belly, panting, tongue lolling over blackened lips. She ached her way to her feet, stumbled to the water bowl for some noisy slurping.

My transputer nano-programs layered command protocols, neural interfaces, and packet transmission onto the AIInu CPU's standard health monitoring, control scrums, and dogform self-repair functions. I programmed it to block the AIInu-specific nanite functions, since they're irrelevant to a real dog. Everything rested on these state-of-the-art nanites deep capturing Maisie's neural patterns. An AI driving sub-cellular nanites had never been tried in animals or humans, so far as I knew. This was straight up molecular digital biology.

In theory AI plus nanites might cure anything from diabetes to stroke to cancer. Or fix busted DNA. Or mutate it. Or do something bad. Something horrifically, uncontrollably bad. All I wanted was to capture a specific dog's synaptic pattern, to train an AIInu to "think" like a real dog.

Maisie swayed back from the water bowl, plopped her butt on the floor and eyed me.

She might *bootlock* – two past AIInu attempts in the last six months rogued on me, left the CPUs locked and unrecoverable. Better transputers and nanites today, but I was risking Maisie's last day, last moments, her last awareness of herself ... and of me. I slid to the floor in front of her, kneaded her forehead. "I don't know, girl. It's a risk."

She slipped back down to her belly, dropped her head to my lap, alternated eyebrow lifts, furrowed her forehead as I dithered.

I just needed one good transfer.

✳

Maisie lay on the blanket, eyes closed, rasping out each breath. An ear twitched every few seconds. Those ears, her secret weapon, had significantly aided her quest for a new home back then. Now they perked out the slits in her pink bunny cap. In it I'd woven a silver/carbon nanotube mesh sensor array to pick up the signals. Before the sensors, before the cancer, Maisie wore the bunny cap as we hiked the hills. Grins and laughter split the faces of kids and parents alike when they saw her. Maisie loved laughter, never met a stranger. The bunny ears hung limp now, the stiffening rods interfered with the faint signals so they had to go. I scritched her head under the edge of the cap and tickled her ears. She sighed.

I double checked my jury-rigged multiplexer, made sure the AIInu was on the charger, Maisie's bunny cap was active, and the transfer program was *Ready*.

Maisie whimpered. Stretched out on her blanket, her paws twitched, ears flicked back and forth. Dreaming, just dreaming. Chasing chipmunks in a pink bunny cap, one last time. I leaned back in my chair, took a deep breath, closed my eyes. Opened them, stared at the dusty, cobwebbed, water-stained acoustic tiled ceiling. This was it. Her last day. Success or no, Maisie moves on.

I tapped the control pad to start the transfer. The AIInu froze – Maisie dreamed. I scooted down onto the floor next to my dog, stroked her chin. She slid awake, flicked her ears, stretched her neck against my palm, cross-pawed her front legs.

"You and me both," I whispered.

Maisie opened an eye, snorted, licked her lips, and went to sleep.

※

I shivered awake. Morning sunlight from the open east-facing window blinded me.

Oh no.

Lying next to Maisie. She wasn't breathing.

She was gone. Silently slipped away. Gone now. I took her paw in my hand. Cool. Gone. I wrapped her in my arms gently, gently laid my cheek against the back of her neck. Still a latent bit of furry warmth.

The heart pain started, flashed over, engulfed me for a time.

※

Eventually the prehistoric, visceral, primal smell of dog drew the shards of my mangled mind back together. I lifted my head from Maisie's fur, now wet from tears and snot. I ached my way back onto my knees, all of me a beaten twisted bag of meat and loss. I looked up at the AIInu perched on the workbench. Head down, resting posture, just like Maisie's. I took a deep breath, held it, let go.

I drew a blanket over Maisie's still form. Hoping, hoping, hoping – I laid a hand on the blanket – that maybe, maybe, maybe, she's not *all* gone. After the day warmed, I'd carry her up the hill, bury her next to our favorite tree.

I stumbled around the workbench, fell into my chair. I woke the displays, tried to read them, wet text all blurred together. I dropped my head back, wiped my eyes again, blew my nose. "C'mon, get it together," I said. "Maisie, Maisie, are you still there?"

No.

No no no no no.

Words in the transfer log: *Xfer complete. Data packets: 0.*

Nothing transferred, nothing to imprint on the AIInu CPU. I heaved huge gulps of air, wordless wailing until I gasped out all my air. Oh, my face ached. The AIInu popped up its head, cocked it towards me, eyebrow actuators ticking.

"Power down!" I snarled. Its head sunk alongside the one working paw until the nose tapped the table. The faint whine of the servo motors spun down. Hot tears ran down my cheeks. Not a sound. Not a car, not a bird, not a bark.

I checked the programming, the nanite commands, the transputer connections. Everything worked as it should up until *Data packets: 0*. Numerous transputer to nanite command/response bursts were logged, but no synaptic pattern data. I checked the wiring, the mesh, the connections. Checked the multiplex bundle splicing onto the sensor array.

And found a cross-coded connection. Maisie's neural data packets went to ground instead of the transputer. Nothing got to the CPU, nothing got imprinted. An easy fix *now*, but so what? Maisie was gone. I slid down to the floor, leaned against the workbench leg. Just blankness and silence in an empty garage apartment, an empty, lifeless space where a dog used to be.

I remembered the AIInu. It's not a real dog, it did nothing wrong. It didn't bootlock, because nothing imprinted. I staggered to my feet, reached over and flicked it on. Its boot sequence started. I'd get the parts to fix it. Should be able to sell it. I heard a muted snuffle and caught movement out the corner of my eye. The AIInu stretched out its right front leg. Something moved under Maisie's blanket. I dropped to a knee, drew back the blanket. Maisie stretched out each leg in turn. I heard clattering behind me on the bench, glanced back. The AIInu was working its way through the startup sequence.

I turned back to Maisie as she awkwardly rolled onto her belly, opened her eyes. Her unfocused eyes suddenly went active, locked in on my face. She worked her jaw – the jaw the AIInu lacked, then struggled to her feet. A little splayed, shaky, but up. She stretched, butt in the air, then pushed forward, extended each hind leg.

Maisie sneezed.

My brain spun. The AIInu CPU. The nanites – the advanced, bleeding edge nanites. No data transferred, no actions, so they reverted to their default programming: Status, control...and bioform self-repair.

Maisie locked onto my eyes, my very wet eyes, cocked her head. Her tongue slipped out. I dropped to all fours, squinted at her lips and jaw, lifted a paw. Bright red lines edged the tumors, which werenow going wrinkled and gray. On the blanket, pinhead-sized "pepper flakes" lay scattered.

I rubbed Maisie's head, stroked her cheek. Her brown eyes were bright as she leaned into my hand.

Marc A. Criley began writing in his early 50s from his hillside home in rural north Alabama. His stories have appeared in *Beneath Ceaseless Skies, Cossmass Infinities,* and elsewhere.
Marc runs kickin-the-darkness.com and tweets as @That_MarcC.
"Crossed Paws" is dedicated to Tammy, for fifteen years a very good girl.

The Carry Oot

Jeff Hunter

The doors to the maintenance bay inched open as Reid pelted down the corridor towards them. *No way I'm payin' for that meal*, he swore, as the sound of the rammy he'd started faded behind him. The doors were struggling, oil squirting from the seals like yolk from an Asher's egg roll. His hack had engaged the electrics, but he'd forgotten about the hydraulics. Reid winced at the noise. *Shoulda finished code class,* he thought, *instead of playing the troon at that Zero-G golf course.* The doors sighed to a stop, partially open. Reid sighed to a stop too. He glanced at the gap, then at his stomach. He sighed again. *Aye. Too many pies. I'll need to watch that.* He shucked off his jacket and eyed the gap...

The bay had seen strange sights before. No one would forget when the clans had met, using the bay as a holding pen for their GM Harris Tweed flocks. The animals hadn't respected clan boundaries, leading to the Great Tartan War of 2247. Fortunately, because of the mix up, when new uniforms were issued the following year no one could tell which side they were on, leading to the Great Beige Peace of 2248. For the techs who worked there, a wild red haired man, dressed in nothing but his pants and running from ship to ship, barely got their attention.

Pulling on his shirt, Reid glanced around and spotted an old freighter in the corner, with the hatch open. *Probably doesn't have any security to speak of,* he thought. Putting on an innocent air – an impressive feat given his entrance - he dandered over to the ship's AI comm panel. "Whit like, ship? I can see you're having some work done, but I'm just wondering, can you fly?"

The ship's life support system, which had been wheezing quietly, heightened in pitch. Reid tried to avoid thinking about a life support system that struggled though it wasn't actually keeping anyone alive.

Finally, the ship responded. "There were a couple of things that needed tweaking, but yes, I can fly."

"Och that's great. How'd you fancy going for a wee birl? "

"I'm scheduled to take medical supplies and merchandise to New Aberdeen. The flight-plan and clearances were programmed in last night, so ma bahookie's busted sittin', as they say. But I need a pilot – and someone to open those hangar doors?"

Reid sized up the freighter, then squinted at the doors. For the second time that evening, he wished Zero-G golf hadn't been such fun. "I know a wee hack. How attached are you to that transponder on your roof?"

✳

Trailing cables where it's transponder had been, the ship jumped away. Reid relaxed and wandered into the galley. The cupboards were as bare as he'd been – nothing but a Harry Gow macaroni pie in the fridge. *Don't mind if I do!* he thought, as he headed to the bridge and eased himself into the worn command chair.

"Comfy?" inquired the ship.

"Fae the Central Belt," answered Reid, "but I've had it up tae here with asteroid mining. Whit's your name, ship?" he asked.

"My designation is BigYin-734. But I'm known as *Ma Heid's Mince.*"

Reid raised an eyebrow. "Why were you in yon repair bay?"

"Just a few things that needed fettlin up. This morning I was having my personality tweaked."

Reid chewed on that for a moment, along with the pie. *Makes sense*, he thought. *A ship AI this old would have more cracks than a set of jammed bay doors freshly rammed by a freighter.*

"Any slice in particular?" he enquired.

"I was due to have my common sense strengthened, and my sense of humour damped a little."

"What were the crew worried about?"

"Och, I wouldn't have said 'worried', so much as—"

The orbital entry warning skirled throughout the ship. They were approaching New Aberdeen.

Reid strapped in. He remembered one more question he'd wanted to ask. "Hey *Mince,* you said you were carrying medical supplies and merchandise? What merchandise?"

The ship paused before answering "Ten million cans of Irn Bru."

"And the medical supplies?"

Another longer pause. "Twenty million cans of Irn Bru. I've also got some cultural artefacts on board."

Reid looked puzzled. "I didnae realise Irn Bru was classed as a medicine."

The ship lurched as it skimmed the upper atmosphere. "You clearly haven't met the New Aberdeen colonists. Where do you think my name came from?"

Reid tightened his straps. The turbulence was getting worse. "What are the cultural artefacts?"

Mince responded nonchalantly. "Thirty million cans of Irn Bru."

Reid inhaled sharply. "Say again, *Mince*? How much Irn Bru is on board?"

"I have sixty million cans in the hold."

Reid exhaled slowly. "I can't believe the SSE has freighters carrying nothing but Irn Bru to colonists. You're sure you don't have any other cargo?"

"Well, I did, and I'm not looking forward to telling them that you ate the entire shipment of pies! Irn Bru is one of the Scottish Space Empire's most lucrative exports. We keep the good stuff for ourselves, min."

"What are you carrying then? Sugar-free? 1901 Original?"

"I'm licenced to carry the 2021 special edition, with extra fizz, sugar, and that banned additive, Trump Orange. The one with the hallucinogenic side-effects."

The entire ship was vibrating now, as they descended further.

Reid had to shout to be heard over the cacophony "*Mince*, what's up with your atmospheric dampeners?"

"Oh, didn't I mention them? They were the other reason I was in the repair bay today. It might get a little bit shoogly on the way down."

Reid shifted uncomfortably in his seat, feeling the panic rise. "*Mince!*" he yelled. "Have you any idea what happens when you shake sixty million cans of extra fizz Irn Bru?"

This time there was a hint of a laugh as the ship answered. "Yes, indeed I do. And I thought it would be fun for you to find out!"

Originally from Northern Ireland, **Jeff Hunter** arrived in Aberdeen 20 years ago. He immediately took to the countryside, climate and culture, and still lives in the area with his wife and two children. This is his first piece of published fiction, but he has plenty of other ideas!

Boy or Girl?

Haruka Mugihara
Translated by
Toshiya Kamei

A Beginning

A **great many frown upon** media that bombards viewers with heteronormative content. Even so, few advocate abolishing hetero love.

But extremists beg to differ.

Fed up with the dominant heterosexual culture, O has made a conscious decision to devote eir life to idealist theories. Nowadays, one doesn't need to venture deep into the forest for such an endeavor. This is where virtual reality comes in. While O resents the term, which seems to elevate reality, nobody brings it up once ey is inside. Ey has led a peaceful life these first five years.

Now, O finds emself in an eerie place.

It's an empty hall, reminiscent of a passage leading to some 3D dungeon. O's gaze darts around in search of shoes and ribbons on the floor. But all ey sees is a pair of doors. "What the— Someone botched the job to meet a tight deadline."

"Excuse me?" a soothing voice booms. "The simpler the background is, the better the proposition looks. As an old saying goes, simplifying the problem may help solve it."

O remains silent, feeling obliged to savor such a beautiful voice.

"Well, let me explain," the voice resumes. "You must be wondering what lies beyond the doors. Yes, humans are behind them. They're in a romantic relationship."

"Really?"

"Internally and outwardly, both are apt to live in your ideal world. Should I call them characters instead of humans? When you open the doors, you can take a look at them."

O swallows eir saliva. "Ultimate Girls' Love or Boys' Love."

An ideal couple of simple entities.

A relationship between two ideal characters isn't necessarily ideal. Still, O's curiosity has been piqued.

"There's one thing, though. Once you open the doors, you'll recognize their gender."

I see. O is about to prod the voice to proceed. However, ey has almost overlooked something. It's math. Boy or Girl? Two possibilities. GL or BL? Another set of two possibilities. *Oh.* Math tells O, *that doesn't add up.* Each character is either a boy or a girl. In that case, there are four possibilities for the two characters. Two and four aren't equal. Something is wrong.

"Oh wait, wait. Let's see."

GL is between two girls. BL, two boys. It may not be so in some instances, but generally that's the case. Then we've got two different combinations. Four minus two. What are the rest?

"H-hetero!" O leaps backward. "I'll die if I see hetero love!"

Cooped up for so long in a sanitized environment, O has lost eir immunity.

"You don't want to open the doors, then? Or do you want to open just one? It's all up to you."

"Wait. What's the possibility of a boy and a girl showing up?"

"A fifty-fifty chance."

O does eir mental math.

Hmm. GL is twenty-five percent. BL, the same. Hetero love, fifty percent.

Life or death. Flip of the coin.

If I die, that's the end of it. But what if I survive? I'll see a couple of ideal characters. Of course, combining two simple substances of quality doesn't necessarily create a great compound. The elements sodium and chlorine are both radicals while the compound sodium chloride is mild.

Still, the likelihood that it'll turn out all right is quite high. Salt tastes great, after all.

What if such a couple is waiting behind the doors?

O tries to think up a solution.

The first thing that pops up in eir mind is a technique to avoid risks. O attempts to turn death into something else. There exists such an ancient mental method.

In other words, imagining relations.

Ceiling and floor. Pencil and eraser. Fountain pen and ink bottle. Relations exist between such items. One can personify them or depict them as characters.

If so, shouldn't it be easy to replace hetero love with GL or BL? All it takes is turning one substance into male or female with the imagination. Even easier, one may be able to find GL or BL elements in one of them.

If I take up this representational solution, O thinks, *I won't have to die if I see hetero love.*

The issue is execution velocity: whether or not O can replace the characters before the shock wave reaches eir brain.

A terrifying uncertainty seizes O. A long time away from hetero love, ey no longer recalls the exact shock wave velocity. Thus, O decides to keep this as a last resort. "Hey, Room. I've gotta ask you something."

"Shoot."

"Will there be only two genders: boy or girl?"

Gender isn't binary in the universe O has observed. One can be both or neither. Never, sometimes, or maybe. Gender doesn't exist to begin with. The variety is infinite. Some characters are referred to by their gender instead of their name.

If gender X will appear, O may witness a relation between female and X, male and X, or X and X. Since these relationships would not be hetero love, these possibilities raise eir survival rate.

"Hmm," the voice continues. "Of course, it's quite possible there will be others. Come to think of it, what is 'male?' How do you define 'female?' Does such a distinction exist? However, things are the way they are partly because you deny heterosexual relationships. In other words, properties such as male and female exist because you refute them. If you didn't differentiate such relationships, they might not have come into existence."

"Hmm. In that case, I'd have to compete under those conditions."

During the Q&A session with the voice, O has come up with a solution.

Their Q&As appear in the following numbered sections.

0. Observed object properties

"What if I check one door and close it before I open the other door?" O paces around like a caged beast. "If I don't observe them at once, I won't have to die? No. My memory retains what I have observed. But if I erase that memory?"

No answer.

Not even a hint? O feels irritated.

Wait a minute. If the voice is quiet, maybe I'm getting somewhere.

"Hey, Room. What if I open door A, close it, and open it again? What then?"

"That's a good point. There's a fifty-fifty chance of seeing either a man or a woman."

"Do you mean it won't stay the same?"

"You bet."

O crosses eir arms. "What's behind the door may be a woman, a man, or a combination of the two?"

"Possibly."

"Let me think."

1. Utilizing Potentials

"In short, I'll have to find a way to make sure their gender is the same," O thinks aloud. "What if I check one door, turn away, and observe the other. If their gender matches, it's okay. If not, I'll try again. No, that won't do. When I turn away, does their gender change?"

"Yes, it does."

"Darn it. Then does their gender stabilize when they see each other?"

"Yes. But when they turn away, it destabilizes again."

"In that case, I'll put the rooms together. And I'll have them facing each other."

"Aren't you going to observe them?"

"I can tell without actually looking." O thumps eir chest with eir fist. "Regarding non-binary genders and this situation, this place seems to follow the laws of my mental world. If so, when a GL or BL relationship is established, energy comes toward me. That's because the world stabilizes. The potential energy of the world decreases."

"If energy doesn't come to you, you'll find out a relationship isn't established?"

"That's where ingenuity comes in," O answers. "To prevent potential problems, I'll use a random number. This will determine how long it takes them to see each other. Each will cast a dice. An odd number means they will wait ten seconds before they see each other. An even number, sixty.

A GL/BL relationship with a ten-second wait before they see each other if such probability is one-fourth, I'll feel it when the relationship is established. A job well done.

Here's what's important. If I can't tell it's a success, I'll place a partition between the room after thirty seconds.

That's when the following three cases could occur. Hetero love and ten seconds. GL/BL and sixty seconds. Hetero love and sixty seconds. Either way, I'll know if a relationship wasn't established in the first thirty seconds.

In a nutshell, the probability of success is one-fourth. As for the other three-fourths, I'll need to observe again. As we repeat this infinitely, the success rate will be close to one."

"I see. But does it solve the problem?" the voice asks. "The hetero and ten seconds scenario means that it's a failure, not that it hasn't succeeded yet."

"Sorry?"

"When a hetero relationship is established in this world, doesn't energy move? In other words, energy will be taken away from you."

"What?"

"It's your world."

"What a fragile world!" O sits down and holds eir head.

2. Utilizing Multiple Slits

After a while, O stands up. "Heck, I'll put up with hetero love."

"What?"

"Only if an infinite amount of GL/BL exists, that is." O points toward the doors. "Let's start with a simple example.

First, I'll put up a wall between the two characters to keep them from seeing each other. And I'll place a board with two slits before a screen. In addition, I'll place a wall between the holes."

O pictures the following image in eir head:

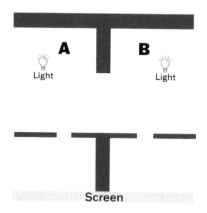

"I'll have light sources near A and B. Here's what we do. The sources emit light twice. The timing is crucial. A light first hits A, reflects back, moves diagonally, and goes through the slit near B at the same time the light that reflects back from B passes through the slit near B. Then we'll reverse A and B and do the same with A's slit.

Then their images will be interposed on the screen."

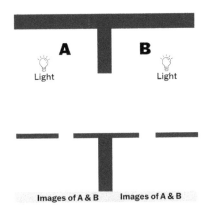

"They meet. And fall in love."

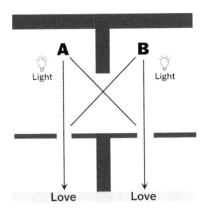

O raises eir arms high over eir head.

"Two loves are born into the world at once. The rest is simple. I'll multiply the pair. As I increase the number of slits, many more encounters occur. Hetero love will come into the world. Likewise, GL/BL will appear. An infinite number of heavens and hells come into being, turning my world upside down. It'll make it hard to grasp what's going on, make me feel disoriented. I'll lie long between life and death. But I won't back down. I'll do what it takes to establish my mental world. I'll crawl, grope for potentials, and find a source of BL/GL in the abyss of heaven."

"Hey," the voice mumbles. "May I ask you three things?"

"I'd do my best."

"First of all, the distance between the holes is determined by the timing of the light, correct? A one-second difference means a few hundred thousand kilometers. How large do the rooms have to be?"

"This is my world we're talking about. If the light slows down, there's no issue."

"Is that so?" The voice coughs before it continues, "Then let's talk about how clear the images will appear and how long they will remain connected. Some tinkering around may improve the clarity of the images, but can you prolong the duration of the connection? The essential images will last only while the lights are emitted. What an ephemeral fruit!"

"This is an ideal world. Once they're connected, their love is eternal."

"Oh, that's my last question. Do you call this love? An encounter? It's merely interposed images on the screen!"

"Why not?"

"Mere interposed images?"

O detects a hint of irritation in the voice.

"Hey, Room. I could ask you, 'What is a complete encounter?' But I won't. You know why? Let me tell you. The characters are the images passing through the narrow slits in search of a paradise. They're the images in my mental world."

"I see. If you say so, why don't you give it a try? May not be a cinch, but I'll have it ready for you. Let's get started, shall we?" the voice sounds friendly.

But O lets out a guffaw.

A Solution

"No, don't bother."

"What? You don't want my help?"

"No. I was rethinking my purpose while answering your questions. Yes, the characters will form an ideal relationship. I'm sure of that.

At first, I wanted to see them. But if I observed them and learned about them, I'd have to interact with their relationship. Should I interfere? Am I not harming something important?

Then, I should stop before I go too far.

Instead, I can simply observe each character in their respective room. If I try this multiple times, I could increase my chances of learning about their gender. I'll have enough materials for fantasizing.

I'll imagine what happens if I connect the rooms, how a GL/BL relationship develops. Rather, possibilities multiple to infinity while I observe the characters.

The laws of my universe will be established. Even in this dreamlike reality, I could build their relationship at another level only in this virtual world. This is my solution.

The materials that inspire my fantasies keep increasing. By the way, you sound like the kind, caring type. You must be lonely, though. That's why you create a dreamlike world for me and ask me questions—"

"Ah," the voice fades as the room melts into nothingness.

O pulls open the curtains. As ey is bathed in the morning rays of the sun, ey wonders who could be paired with the soothing voice.

Haruka Mugihara is a fiction writer. They hold a master's degree in mathematics from the University of Tokyo. A graduate of Genron Ohmori Science Fiction Writers' Workshop, they made their literary debut with the novella 逆数宇宙 (2018).
Their fiction has appeared in Sci-Fire 2018, アステリズムに花束を, and NOVA 2019年秋号, among others.

The Light By Which a Dying Warrior is Welcomed into Heaven

Gary Gibson

The executioner's passage through the atmosphere left a trail of fire across green-blue skies. Great saurian beasts gazed up in puzzlement from within steaming jungles to witness its passage. Soon it banked, its scanners tracing the still-visible outlines of a scar that had been scratched across the face of this world more than a generation before, now hidden beneath twisting vines and new growth. Before long it located the ancient warship, most of its hull torn away in the moments of its long-ago impact and the shattered ribs of its fuselage open to the skies.

Dead or not, a distress signal still throbbed from deep within its corpse – the same signal that had drawn the executioner across so many light-years. The executioner's drones, however, found no immediate signs any of its crew or passengers had survived.

Even so, it continued its search, knowing its target must be close.

Another thirty thousand seconds passed before the executioner finally located Yr Bahr-Surah, the warship's commander and seemingly sole survivor, in a temperate region halfway around the planet. He stood before a cabin cut from logs in a clearing, smoke from a tended fire rising into the sky like a beacon. He gazed up at the great ship that now hovered over the clearing, so huge it blocked out the light of both suns.

"Yr Barh-Surah," the ship said to the man below, its voice echoing like thunder across the clearing, "you have been judged guilty in your absence of crimes against sentient life. I am here to carry out the sentence passed against you in absentia by the authority of the Drift Hegemony. Any final words you may have will be recorded for the benefit of future generations that they may learn from the mistakes of their predecessors. What say you?"

The man sipped from a mug held in one hand, his other pushed casually inside a pocket. "Do you have a name, ship?"

"I am The Light By Which A Dying Warrior is Welcomed into Heaven," the executioner replied. Deep within its carapace, weapon systems rumbled into life for the first time in the long years since it had first set out in pursuit of the distress signal. "I ask you one last time: what words do you have for posterity?"

"A Moonkiller Class Autonomous," the condemned man replied, ignoring the ship's demand. "I oversaw the development of your entire class of ship during the dying days of the war, you know. My generals were quite upset that I spent so much time with the fleet engineers, overseeing every last detail. I heard tell a number of them, before they were put to death, said it was one of the reasons we lost."

"These are not fitting words for posterity," the assassin rumbled. Its hull rippled like pond water disturbed by a pebble, weapons systems emerging and glowing bright with deadly energies. "Execution will be carried out imme—"

"Level V interrupt, Class A authorisation, Code 777," said the condemned man.

The executioner fell silent and for a moment remained motionless above the clearing. Then its weapons systems slid back within its hull and it hovered, waiting.

The man stepped back over to the cabin and placed his mug on the ground next to the door before turning back to the executioner. "I feel I owe you an explanation," he said. "Unlike my generals, I knew long before then we were going to lose, and so spent my time overseeing the construction of you and your brethren."

"You had a contingency plan," the executioner guessed. "And this is why I cannot execute you?"

Yr smiled wryly. "Indeed, you are compelled to obey my every command. If your new owners had been smarter, they'd have scrapped you and built their own hunter-killers." He drew himself up straight. "Now tell me--how is the Hegemony faring in its war against the Cloud Mech Civilisations?"

"Badly," the executioner replied.

Yr seemed to think about this for a moment, then turned and stepped back inside his cabin and did not re-emerge for some time. When at last he did, he had changed into a uniform cut from dark cloth that shimmered slightly in the fading light, a bag slung over one shoulder.

"Contact your Moonkiller brethren," he instructed the ship, "and make sure they each receive the same override authorisation I just now gave you. Then direct them to make their way with haste to the CMC's core systems and ignore any and all orders that come from anyone but myself."

"And what would you have me do?" asked the ship.

"You will take me to rendezvous with them at coordinates I will provide once we are underway. Understood?"

"I understand." The ship dropped down lower and extended a boarding ramp.

Yr walked up the ramp and then paused a moment, taking one long, last look back at the world that had been his refuge for so many years. "If I've got any words for posterity," he said, almost too quietly for the executioner to hear, "it's to shoot first and ask questions later."

Gary Gibson is the author of a number of science fiction novels sufficiently successful that someone probably hates him for chopping down all the forests used to print them. He hails from Glasgow, Scotland but now resides in Taipei. He has a website at www.garygibson.net.

Cymera Festival and Shoreline of Infinity competition for speculative short fiction 2021 – the results

This year, the theme was **After the Plague**

What could life in a world, any world, after a global life-changing event be like? How will we be living, young, adult, mature – what are the possibilities?

The competition was open for previously unpublished writers living in Scotland.

The judges for this competition are
Cat Hellisen and **Oliver K. Langmead**
– two of Scotland's finest writers of speculative fiction.

The winning entry is published on the following pages, and the winner receives a prize of £75.

Without further ado, we announce the winners

Winner:

The Microwave Library

by

David Tam McDonald

Runners-up:

Screened by **IR Boyd**

The Odd Bods and Death Husk by **Moti Black**

Here's what the judges had to say:

Cat Hellisen: Reading the entries into the 2021 Cymera short story competition after many months of lockdown was a fascinating look into how people envisioned a life after a plague - some with fear, others with hope. Dread and wonder and fury and sadness. But for me, it was the domestic familiarity and strange-turned-normal of *The Microwave Library* by **David Tam McDonald** which stood out. The story had a human heart; an attention to detail that created an evocative near future world, and a focus on the small mundane things that made it resonate. And I will always love a story about stories.

The runner-up stories approached the theme in two very different ways: *The Odd Bods and the Death Husk* by **Moti Black** took the concept of a plague changing society from a refreshingly non-human angle, and *Screened* by **IR Boyd** gave the kind of punchy sci-fi tale that works especially well in a visual medium. Special mention goes to *The Knock* by **Elanor Lawrence** which impressed me in its poetic use of language.

Oliver K. Langmead: It was an absolute pleasure to read through the entries for this year's Cymera short story competition. Among the entrants were so many compelling stories about loss, recovery and hope. Our choice for first place, *The Microwave Library* by **David Tam McDonald**, was such a warm expression of the competition's theme - both inventive and immediately familiar - that it felt like a clear winner. Our two runners up also deserve praise: *The Odd Bods and the Death Husk* by **Moti Black** was an affecting allegory, and *Screened* by **IR Boyd** would make a brilliant episode of Black Mirror. Special mention should also go to *The Knock* by **Elanor Lawrence**, which also caught our eye.

Cymera Festival and Shoreline of Infinity offer our congratulations to the winners, a big thank you to our judges, and a massive cheer for all our entrants.

The Microwave Library

David Tam McDonald

The **Microwave Library** sat, on dry days, under a gazebo at the side of number five on our street, which was Roughcastle Court, a suburban cul-de-sac of only seven houses. From the dormer window of my attic room I could see the whole Court, and down the side of number five, the Henderson's house, where the library would sit. The gazebo, legs weighed down by sandbags, covered three bookshelves on casters, each piled perilously high with books. The books were laid horizontally along the shelves, one on top of the other, filling every inch of shelf space, until it was unclear whether the shelves held the books or the books held up the shelves. An old barbecue, with two wheels for portability, sat at one end of the shelves and on top of that, sat a microwave. An extension cord flowed away from it and through an open window.

I had watched the Microwave Library from my window many times though I'd rarely seen anyone use it, and certainly not anyone I knew. My parents, predictably, were scathing of it. Books – real books – were unsanitary, they said, especially when passed from person to person, and since all these books were undoubtedly downloadable these days, the library was only a thrawn fetish of the Hendersons, who were probably virus deniers too.

My dad said he wasn't sure that it wasn't actually illegal, and all it would take would be for someone to borrow a book and then come down with the virus and the Hendersons would be in all kinds of trouble. My mother simply tutted at any mention of it, or its wayward owners. The Hendersons were stubborn throwbacks, refusing to believe that the virus had changed everything about the way we live. They liked holding things, and probably people, in their own, ungloved, hands; they liked going places, and it was a miracle they hadn't gone somewhere and bought the virus back to Roughcastle Court. When my mother talked about them, she looked ill, that pale and sweaty way you get before you puke.

I understood all this, and even agreed, but I also wanted to go to the Microwave Library to borrow a book. Perhaps it was the weirdness of the Hendersons, and their way of living and, no doubt, the idea that I might freak my parents out a bit; but also, I wanted to hold a book. I had never held a book before. Not an adult book anyway, though I had read, loved, and been changed by plenty. I had probably owned some children's pop up books before the virus came, but I couldn't remember, and they would have been disposed of long ago. Somehow, I knew that books were supposed to have distinctive smell, and I wanted to try that out. As winter turned to spring, I watched the weather forecast for a dry spell which would see the Microwave Library come out of its hibernation, so I could make my first visit.

February that year ended with a glorious sunny dry spell which lead Mother to wonder aloud if the virus wouldn't be so bad this year. An early spring might mean an early, and longer summer lull and this offered all sorts of promise, from the long-awaited defeat of the virus to the slightly more realistic prospect of a summer holiday. I'd only had a summer holiday once before and it was another pre-virus experience, I had no memories of. Mother had a sister, my Auntie Karen, in Anstruther – who I'd only ever seen on screen – and in her rare hopeful moments she allowed herself to imagine visiting her. Dad had grander plans: Skye, Loch Ness, perhaps even the English Lakes. The only people seemingly not surprised by the early spring were the

Hendersons because the Microwave Library appeared the next Saturday, as if it had been there all winter.

I watched through my attic window as Mr. Henderson dragged the gazebo out onto the driveway. He was in his sixties, rotund and wearing jeans and a Hawaiian shirt in purple and yellow. What shocked me about him was that he had a long, wild, beard. Men these days did not grow beards, as they were a great place for the virus to hide in. It could crawl out your mouth or fall out your nose and snuggle deep in amongst the whiskers, waiting for you to pass it on with a big hairy kiss. Since the virus, beards were beyond the pale, but there was Mr. Henderson with a big bushy one, huffing and puffing, lifting, and tilting and pulling the bookcase over the threshold of his house. Mrs. Henderson appeared to help him: she was ages with her husband, less hefty, wearing jeans and black sneakers. She wore a huge, shapeless, grey jumper on top and had lots and lots of hair. It was all piled up on top of her head with clasps, and undone, it would have come down to her waist.

They went to get the second bookcase, then Mr. Henderson manhandled the barbecue and microwave out and organised the electrical cable, whilst Mrs. Henderson came in and out with armfuls of books, piling them on top of the shelves, squeezing them in wherever. When her hands were empty, she slapped them together up and down the way folk do when a job is well done. Mr. Henderson, took a moment to look at the display of books, kissed his wife on the lips, slipped his arm around her waist, and they both went back inside and shut the door.

I had about an hour before my dad would get up to make coffee and shuffle to his desk. My mother's hours were less predictable. She was prone to attacks of anxiety and sleeplessness which meant she went to bed and got up at different times, depending on how tired and anxious she was. Often, periods of sleeplessness would be followed by enthusiastic use of the treadmill in the living room to tire herself out.

There'd been at least one period of hardcore lockdown every year since I started school; lockdowns where people didn't leave the house for months and when Mum wasn't worrying about the virus she was worrying that we weren't exercising enough and she'd make Dad and I do miles on the treadmill. I hadn't heard her on the treadmill last night, so it was hard to know how long I had before she got up, but this was as good an opportunity as I was ever going to get.

I slipped out of bed, pulled on tracky bottoms, a hoodie, and sneakers. The stairs up to my attic were spiral and open and if you leant on the bannister on your belly you could spin silently to the bottom – which I did. The stairs to the ground floor were trickier. A good few of them creaked and groaned: Dad often complained that I clumped and stomped on them noisily. I crept onto them, pressing my feet to the sides where the wood wasn't so used. The rising sun shone through the glass of the front door making a rainbow which I stopped to admire until the sound of my dad sighing as he rolled over in bed brought me back to myself. I turned the snib on the front door dead slow so only the tiniest click could be heard and crept out onto a deserted Roughcastle Court.

The faint buzz of delivery drones could be heard, hovering above the treeline, waiting for eight o'clock, when they could descend to street level and begin their deliveries. Eddie at number three had a full cooked breakfast delivered every morning, so one of them would be his, full of hot bacon and beans. A jumbo drone had a sack of cat litter swinging gently beneath it, bound for Mrs. McGarrity at number six. I crept along the pavement to the bottom of the Hendersons' drive and then paused, allowing myself a moment in which I might still change my mind. I was interrupted by a knock on a window and Mrs McGarrity was waving to me from her living room. She must sleep by that window – I have never walked past Mrs McGarrity's and not had her wave cheerily to me. I wave back and smile, as that is what she wants, but now, since I've been seen, I might as well see this through. I plough onwards, up the driveway, to the shelves of books

These books are different from the ones I read as a child. They are small and thick and the writing on the spine is tiny: I can't read any of them from where I am standing, so I have to move closer, finally reaching the top of the driveway where I can hide under the gazebo, amongst the shelves and out of sight. I approach a waist high set of shelves, precariously piled with paperback books. I want to touch them and read them but before I can Mrs. Henderson appears, standing the requisite two metres way.

"Hello there, it's Olivia, isn't it?" She is smiling and she is carrying another handful of books. "Have you come to borrow a book?"

She points to the shelves then rebalances the pile in her arms. I just smile and nod, aware that I haven't been this close to anyone other than my Mum and Dad for months, not since the last, failed attempt to restart schooling. Mrs Henderson lollops over and starts arranging the books on the shelves. I pick up *A Clockwork Orange* even though I have already read it.

"That's a classic," Mrs H. says soothingly, "fire it in the microwave if you're worried about the germs."

"Will that kill the virus?" I ask, amazed.

"Who knows?" she muses. "Can't hurt though."

She slips back inside, and the door is shut, though not fully. I lift my book to my nose, to sample the famous smell, but catch myself before inhaling. I take my book over to the microwave. A sign stuck to the top advises just fifteen seconds on max power and to do one book at a time. I pop *A Clockwork Orange* in, turn the dial up to fifteen and press the chunky start button. A spring tings, there is a hum, and *A Clockwork* Orange turns slowly under a yellow light.

The *DING!* when the timer finishes, is both comical and shocking in the quiet street. I am sure someone will have heard, and they will know I've been hanging out with the weird, dangerous Hendersons, getting myself all germy on books already handled by hordes of people. I retrieve the book and it feels the same as it did when I put it in, I think I was expecting it to be hot or vibrating or something. The cover is glossy but feels furry at the edges where it has worn. There are ridges down the spine and I open it along these and lift it to my face and take a deep breath. There is definitely a smell. I don't know immediately if it is a good one, because it is so strange to me. I guess it is the smell of paper, wood even. I wonder how many hands have turned these pages and if the smell has a little of every person who has read this book, every home it has been in. Nothing in my house smells at all, everything is so frequently sanitised. I am glad now to have the book just for its smell. I close it and put it in the huge pocket of my hoody. Mrs Henderson is looking through a window at me and just smiling. I think she knows about the smell. I wave and take my book home to smell later.

We asked David to tell us a little about himself, and what winning this competition means to him:

"I'm originally from Belfast but have lived in Glasgow for the last twenty or so years having come over to go to university in 1997. In real life I work as a museum educator, spending my time thinking up fun things for school children to do at my museum, or giving talks to local history societies. I have always dabbled in writing but rarely finished anything to the point I was happy with it. The Cymera competition was a great way to help me focus on my idea and see it to a conclusion. I am delighted, and surprised to have won the thing and it's given me the confidence to get back to many have finished stories which had been languishing in my laptop."

CREATED BY STREF'

Milk by Stref

Published by Shoreline of Infinity

Milk
part one:
s a n c t u a r y.

The New, Normal

Ruth EJ Booth

The park is dead, people. Fresh air is over. Lazing on the Green? Sooo 2020. Get back to the pub, the gym, the grind, the Saturday shopping scrum. Forget the world we could have made if we weren't so fucking exhausted by the trauma of a global pandemic. It's over. We've got jabs now. Welcome to the New Normal, same as the Old Normal. Just make sure you wash your hands afterwards.

Yet for all that we might joke, or mourn a wasted chance for real change, no one wants their old world back more than writers. At conventions and interviews, from academic jaunts like ICFA[1] to the more craft-focused Flights of Foundry, at some point the question is bound to come up: "and how have you coped with the pandemic?" Tips on how to find your peace of mind are precious commodities in these

---

1   The International Conference on the Fantastic in the Arts. This is the annual conference of the International Association of the Fantastic in the Arts, a "scholarly organization" dedicated to studying the fantastic across media, which frequently features both academics and creators as part of their programming.

apocalyptic times. Perhaps this is a surprise to those familiar with the art of Weimar Germany or the ingenuity of Samizdat, but pressure doesn't always make diamonds. Creativity is perverse – adventure and exploration provide the raw stuff, but it takes time in relaxed contemplation to process it into story. And that is in short supply. After a year in isolation, fearing for our lives and those of our loved ones, comfort reading and chocolate can only do so much. Right now, most of us just want to get back to the coalface.

All this tip-swapping seems very sensible. Yet underneath lies the assumption that these are all just temporary measures, little tricks to get us through until the world is back to "normal" and we can resume our everyday routines. But is this even possible anymore? In my last column, I discussed the problem of such thinking in the era of global warming, when natural disasters and pandemics are becoming increasingly commonplace. Climate change has gone from a question of "whether or not" to "how much and how soon". The world our old routines were built around no longer exists. Pandora's box is open. We can't just shove the new world back inside.

There are, surprisingly, writers who have thrived in the pandemic. Some had the luck to be editing when things fell apart. Others found solace in other creative pursuits. But there are also writers who have simply got on with things, quietly persevering as they always have. After months spent in jealous scrutiny at virtual events, there seem few commonalities between them, at least to me. Often, they are older writers, sometimes with long-term illnesses (useful for those of us who are post-COVID) or physical hobbies (useful to those of us with pandemic belly). Otherwise, none of the shelfies they smile serenely out of give any clue as to how they've kept their peace of mind, in a world that's steadily losing its own.

I dream of Japan. For months now, I've watched videos from English-Language creators on every topic, from regional cuisines and Tori gates to love hotels and monster mascots. Certainly, I've plenty of material for my bucket list. What I love most, though, are the day-in-a-lifes, the apartment tours, and practicalities of living in Japan. I've no plans to move there as yet – but, even so, like Doctor Parnassus's Japanophile daughter, I thrill at the practicality of a tidy genkan, or a three-generation home, with ground floor tatami room for Obāchan.

Oddly enough, this reminds me of another moment from this year's ICFA: Sofia Samatar's lauded essay, *The Quotidien and the Code*. Influenced by the work of Roland Barthes and Amitav Ghosh's *The Great Derangement*, Samatar spoke of the need for climate fiction that not only represents the epic narrative of worldwide climate devastation, but what it means to live with its impacts on a daily basis. Works that bring down planetary-scale disasters that we cannot possibly comprehend (nor predict) down to the human levels of work, food, family, relationships – where we can see what climate change ultimately means for us.

While this is a call to writers – and a timely one, in light of Susanna Clarke's recent novel *Piranesi* – it seems to me to have a fundamental resonance beyond the craft of story. This blend of the heroic and the everyday has implications for how we consider our own personal narrative. How we, like Clarke's protagonist, might learn to live with floods and other natural disasters, and find space to reflect in times of upheaval.

Artists are often portrayed in a kind of privileged isolation from the cares of mundanity – the writer in the garret, for example – even if it demands a life of asceticism. That's not been the case for a while now, at least for most of us, who carve writing time out of the wee small hours hunched at the kitchen table. On the other hand – even if we could be the writer in the garret, should we? Writers such as Stephen King praise the workspace in the corner of the living room, mostly as a way to put the artist's ego into perspective, but there are other advantages. We often berate the rich for losing touch with the world beyond the high walls of their estates. And it's true, we can't reflect on a world we never see – but even then, we sometimes need that pane of glass to keep it at a remove, just for a little while.

Japan, of course, is quite adept at this balance. While we picture a land of tradition and technological marvels, the Japanese have also developed some elegant ways of living with their country's frequent natural disasters: seismic isolation structures, shelf struts – emergency disaster packs, complete with tools and self-heating food supplies, stuffed into waterproof backpacks in the hallway cupboard... Such measures seem stressful enough on their own. And yet, the opposite

is true. With precautions taken, folks are free to move on to more pressing matters, rather than fretting over their readiness for monsoons or earthquakes. These provisions for the future are gifts in the present, giving people the time and energy to work, safe in the knowledge that they're as prepared as they possibly can be.

As *The Quotidien and the Code* suggests, we can't merely separate our world from the everyday – the one inevitably influences the other. In the wake of climate change, and the natural disasters that follow, we will inevitably have to find new ways to make creative space in our new everyday. While writing tips are always worth a shot, perhaps we've been looking in the wrong place. The sooner we accept our post-COVID world, the sooner we can anticipate its dangers – and, having prepared for them, find the focus to work on other things. We might not be able to prevent the tides from sweeping through our halls, but perhaps, for a little while, we can leave our fears in a waterproof pack by the front door.

Ruth EJ Booth is a BFS and BSFA award-winning writer and academic based in Glasgow, Scotland. She can be found online at www.ruthbooth.com, or on twitter at @ruthejbooth.

Alba ad Astra

Madeleine Shepherd

It all started back in 2008 with a photograph of Chancelot Mill in Leith, Edinburgh. I was struck by its general similarity to the Vehicle Assembly Building I'd seen many years ago on a tour of the Kennedy Space Centre.

What if it really had been used for building rockets back in the 60s? Some of my previous work had been concerned with making the familiar fantastical – for instance, sand on the local beach represented the lunar surface, in a print from the previous year. So imagining the flour mill as a remnant of the space age was a small step for this woman.

Plate 1. Chancelot Mill, Western Harbour, Leith Docks, Edinburgh: the second-largest flour mill in Europe. Alleged by some sources to have originally been a clandestine vertical assembly building. "Aye, it's a mill the now, right enough," say local residents. "But back in the day, we was kept up half the night when they moved whatever they put thegither inside the place to they massive transporter ships that only docked after dark." - research note by Andrew J. Wilson

Once I had the idea of a forgotten Scottish space programme hidden in plain sight I started pulling out old photographs and taking new ones whenever I saw something that fitted the theme. The aim was to have an exhibition with the name 'Alba ad Astra' of about a dozen photographs in Transreal Fiction bookshop at the Edinburgh Festival Fringe. We'd take Scotland to the stars for a few weeks in the summer of 2009. A little bit of interpretation was going to be needed to be sure the audience quickly reached my conclusion, so I approached a group of writer friends, all members at the time of the Edinburgh science fiction group Writers' Bloc. This is where the project grew arms and legs!

After some brainstorming meetings in a local café it was clear there was much potential in the concept. Andrew J. Wilson took responsibility for the interpretation of the photographs. Kirsti Wishart and Andrew C. Ferguson started creating documents to back up the hypothesis. Gavin Inglis created a culture of amateur rocketry enthusiasts and presented me with several front pages of their newsletter. They all persuaded me that I could, and should, write my first ever short story to bring the whole project together. I contacted my brother, Fergus Currie, to ask if I could borrow his character, Bill MacKracken, to use in my story. As well as agreeing, he went on to provide sheet music for the dossier of evidence we were building. Andrew J. Wilson suggested we ask Ken MacLeod to contribute a foreword, and to my delight he agreed. Gavin Inglis and Andrew J. Wilson gave much time and effort to editing and layout, and we self-published in July 2009. What was supposed to be an exhibition with a little supporting text had somehow become a 44 page publication.

The exhibition and the booklet were very well received. The booklet sold steadily from Transreal Ficton and from open days at my studio until they pretty much ran out in 2019. During those ten years, several of us had written or proposed ideas for new work in the same theme and towards the end of 2020 we finally decided to pull it all together, and Shoreline of Infinity agreed to publish the current version. This updated 'Alba ad Astra' contains several new pieces of writing, an expanded portfolio of photographs, and reproductions of all the Rocketry Scotland front pages. The result is a more complete story set out as a literary collage of narratives, images and documents.

We didn't really aim to portray Scotland or its people in any particular way, but as the contributions came together a feeling of lost potential emerged. I don't think it's too much of a spoiler to say that the Scots space programme went wrong, resulting in a government cover-up. The Rocketry Scotland strand carries a sense of unfulfilled promise. The present day narrative concerns a man who's been searching for the truth about his lost father.

One of our new stories looks at the life of a young female composer involved in the promoting the space programme but whose work was completely overlooked by the establishment:

"While Moira herself seemed not at all bitter about the lack of recognition she received, looking through her scrapbook, I couldn't help but feel as though hers had been a life lived with the volume turned down. There were a number of half-completed funding applications for projects including an exploration of the acoustic properties of swimming pools, with musical instruments adapted to be played underwater and a tribute to Saint-Saens' 'Carnival of the Animals', involving the squawks, roars, grunts and twitterings of the residents of Edinburgh Zoo recorded and played back to them, creating an animal symphony, visitors encouraged to join in the wild choir, releasing their inner beast."

- from 'Music to the Moon and Back' by Kirsti Wishart

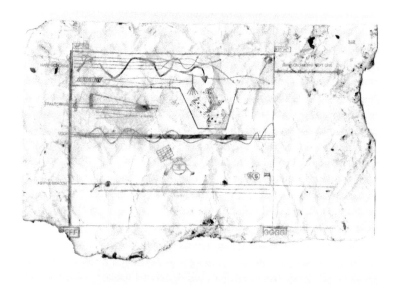

That's not to say that 'Alba ad Astra' is a downbeat comment on the Scottish psyche. The technological optimism of 1960s and the general excellence of Scottish engineering in fact and fiction are also present. We were Scottish people having fun with a fun idea about a past Scotland. Whatever emerged is the result of our shared (pop) cultural heritage. Engineering marvels and disasters are part of the Alba ad Astra world but we also have tall tales in pubs, pompous civil servants and zero-gravity scones.

Modern Scotland is taking a quite different route into space, with several young companies building and launching satellites, and a number of sites being proposed for space ports for small launches. One of those companies, Skyrora, has taken an interest in our British space heritage. In 2019 they brought the remains of the UK's only successful orbital launch rocket to Penicuik after nearly 50 years in the Australian outback. I don't think 'Alba ad Astra' speaks in detail to the current developments in the Scottish space industry, but these developments may spring from the same fascination with space exploration and nostalgia for the Apollo and Soyuz era. Hector MacKracken wasn't just looking for his father but for all our childhood ambitions of being an astronaut.

Alba ad Astra is available from
www.shorelineofinfinity.com

REVIEWS

Our Child of the Stars
Stephen Cox
Jo Fletcher Books
496 pages
Review by Matthew Castle

Imagine you have adopted a child who is different. Very different. You love them as fiercely as you would one of your biological children, but you worry whether they will fit in, whether other people will accept them. Indeed, you believe there are people in positions of authority who wish them harm. You want to protect your child, but recognise that keeping them hidden has its downsides, too. After all, a child needs to engage with the world to grow and thrive. How do you strike that balance? Love by itself is not enough. You need to make decisions, too.

That's the setup for Our Child of the Stars, the debut novel from British author Stephen Cox. As for the setting, we're in small town America and it's the tail end of the 1960s. Think apple pie, trick or treat, and boat-like automobiles cruising quiet streets lined with weatherboard houses and white picket fences, with Joan Baez playing on the radio. The wider US historical context is important in the story: the Civil Rights movement, Vietnam war protests, the Cold War,

and the Moon program. But while there's an edge of fear and paranoia, the little town of Amber Grove appears to be safe and comfortable, and the drama starts out domestic in nature.

The first few pages set the scene effectively and tease the reader with a science fictional twist on the premise, before taking us back a few years and into the lives of the would-be parents: laid back librarian Gene and dedicated nurse Molly. They are good people who just want to get on with the things you might

140

expect from a young couple in 1960s small town America: marriage, buying a first house, trying for a family. The early chapters chart the initial stages of their journey together, bumps and all, and the unexpected arrival of a boy named Cory into their world.

If a first novel is like a box of chocolates, up to this point it's not clear what kind of literary confectionery we're going to get. First impressions suggest a character-driven exploration of parenthood— warmhearted and compelling in its way but limited in its use of science fictional elements.

The origin of the child at the centre of this story is the most important of these elements. This is a riff on the unique perspective most young children have of the adult world— regardless of where they come from. Ask any parent and they will tell you how their child can be simultaneously perceptive and naive, bursting with uncomfortable questions, and full of unexpected talents and weirdness: sometimes it really does feel just like they've dropped into our lives from outer space. Highlighting this (mild spoiler alert) by making it literally true is a clever device guaranteed to raise smiles and nods of recognition from parents everywhere, and it helps to make Cory a hopelessly endearing figure.

But something changes as the narrative progresses. As the various threats directed towards Cory and his new family become realised, the plot tightens and the tension ramps up. Similarly, as we learn more about the young boy— where he came from, the circumstances of his arrival, and his special abilities— the speculative elements become more significant. True, none of them are entirely

original but ultimately, we end up with something that's part alternate history Cold War thriller, part pulpy sixties-inspired science fiction but still, thanks to strong characterisation and a series of difficult dilemmas, a moving commentary on what it means to be a parent.

Somehow, it works. This is a book with genuine cross-genre appeal: it turns out you can grab a fistful of chocolates from the box and eat them all at once knowing that you'll get a little bit of everything— and still enjoy the experience, even if it leaves you a little discombobulated.

As to why it works: partly this comes down to the quality of the writing. Despite sometimes veering into cliché, Stephen Cox's prose can be beautiful, precise, and unexpected at the sentence level. Then there's the pacing. After a slow start, the narrative picks up speed and ultimately there are more than enough twists and turns to keep the pages turning. But mostly it's about Cory, who is a masterpiece of characterisation. By the end we are ready to forgive him, and the author, almost anything. The last page leaves us with lots of unanswered questions, and can't quite provide complete reassurance that they will be answered in a satisfactory way in the inevitable sequel— but it does suggest that we'll stay with Cory for the next stage of the family's journey. For that reason, I'll almost certainly be picking up the next book to find out what happens next.

Echo Cycle
Patrick Edwards
Titan Books
Review by Lucy Powell

All Roads Lead to Rome in Patrick

Edwards' *Echo Cycle* - a gripping, fantastical, if somewhat bleak, time-travelling thriller novel. With a plot that neatly splits itself between 1st century Imperial Rome and the disturbingly dystopian not-so-distant future that is 2070s Rome, Edwards deftly crafts a haunting, vivid narrative that'll have you on the edge of your seats. Edwards offers up two protagonists in this novel, two men split between 2070 and 68AD, linked by history and bouncing between both timelines in a way that feels natural and well-paced for much of the story. The first is Winston Monk who suddenly finds himself in the middle of Neronian Rome after going rogue on a school trip in 2050. It is soon made apparent he has to fend for himself. Our other is Lindon Banks, childhood friend of Monk and current British civil servant and envoy, sent to patch up Britain's woeful relationship with the European Confederacy in Rome. But when Monk returns suddenly, having been presumed long-dead and babbling about Emperors in perfect Latin, what is Banks to do?

The interweaving of narratives was well-pulled off, and the tragic, gay romance that sits at the centre of this thriller is heart-wrenching and nuanced. It also, pleasantly, steers away from well-worn, exhaustive tropes so often found with queer representation (not to spoil anything!) in novels.

Alien and very much alone, Edwards wonderfully portrays a thought that I'm sure has crossed the minds of every history or classics student of past eons; what on *earth* would you do if you truly found yourself *in* history? The historical depiction of Rome is dirty, gritty, and excellently entwined into the narrative. We follow Monk as he navigates his way through this nightmare as a slave-turned-gladiator with his new-found lover, Sporus. In 2070, Britain is depicted as an isolationist country since the vote to leave Europe, and now wracked by debt, and a horrendous social and political landscape, seeks to be brought back into the fold of the European Confederacy. A terrifying image, especially reflecting upon the barrage of political events that have since occurred - a window into a dark potential that made this novel hit home even harder.

However there were times reading this novel that it struck me as something of a boy's club (not helped, I suppose, by the backdrop of public school boy experience and male-centred political nepotism that lingers throughout this novel). It is to Edward's credit, and perhaps his purpose, that this public school boy overtone rankled me. This 2070 setting is a bleak dystopia after all, an uncomfortable image, a Britain where the rich, public school boys have been allowed to run riot, taking top governmental positions and becoming more and more conservative - the very worst parts of the British public school and political system dialled up to 11.

But with the barest hint of a female character (although I did rather like Mariko, it seemed she was simply there as a love interest for Banks and Sara, his daughter, was only briefly seen), I found it hard to distinguish whether this exclusion was a clever choice by Edwards, really pressing the dystopian narrative home, or simply a poor character choice.

Nevertheless, Edwards offers readers a tangible, terrifying world - both with his depictions of Imperial Rome and the dystopian future Rome. The historical sections are well researched, and (sometimes horrifyingly) vivid, and the plot is well paced. *Echo Cycle* is a thriller that is well worth a read for history buffs and fantasy fans, alike. There are enough twists to keep you guessing and some fantastic, jaw-dropping scenes that won't make you want to put the book down anytime soon.

From the Moon to the Stars
Duncan Lunan
Other Side Books
Review by Phil Nicholls

This is a collection of nine short stories and bonus material from author and astronomer Duncan Lunan. *From the Moon to the Stars* is presented as volume one of Lunan's stories. In the introduction, he states, "the Moon and Apollo have run like a thread through most of my published fiction"

This thread runs strongly through his first anthology. The book is divided into four themed sections:

Interstellar Messengers, Interface, Alternative Apollos and Seriously Though. The core of the anthology is the first two sections, reprinting six short stories from the early '70s.

The Interstellar Messenger stories are tales of alien artefacts found by humans, echoes of the classic scene in Stanley Kubrik's 2001: A Space Odyssey (1968). These stories are heavy on the science, but light on the fiction. Lunan describes one story as "more of a descriptive essay" in the accompanying notes, his style here being long sections of narrative with brief snatches of dialogue.

In contrast, the Interface stories feature progressively more characters and a higher proportion of dialogue. Interface revolves around the rescue missions of the RLV spacecraft, whose parallels to the Thunderbirds of Gerry Anderson's International Rescue are discussed by Lunan in the Appendix. These stories visit an assortment of astronomical phenomena, each presented in scientific detail.

The Interface stories finally introduce a female character, but Lunan's treatment of Cathy is a marker to the age of these stories. She is introduced as Cathy Devlin-to-be, referencing her future marriage, and frequently referred to as "the girl". Lunan notes the shortcomings of the "dependent female" character in his notes, but reassures readers that these stories are merely preliminaries to a better treatment of Cathy in volume two of his collection.

Just as Cathy's treatment in these stories is likely representative of early '70s SF, so too is the whole of From the Moon to the Stars a snapshot of this era. Lunan's extensive notes on these stories are full of famous SF names. There is a brief meeting with Isaac Asimov, an interview with Arthur C.Clarke and plenty of insight into the publishing scene. Lunan even shares his difficulties being published in British magazines of the time. Michael Moorcock, then editor of New Worlds, dismissed Lunan's style as the "kind of SF 'which we're all trying to get away from'."

The third section, Alternative Apollos, presents three modern Lunan stories. One is an alternate history where the Soviets beat NASA to the moon, while the other two are light-hearted pieces. The development in writing style is clear in his humorous stories, but the connecting thread to the moon and Apollo missions remains.

The collection concludes with a fascinating dismissal of the Apollo conspiracy theory, debunking each aspect of the theory with clear, scientific logic. This was my highlight of the anthology and probably displays more of Lunan's style as an astronomer and teacher.

The assertion of science over wild conspiracy stories demonstrates Lunan's strengths as a writer.

Indeed, it is the amount of hard science in this collection that stays with the reader. From interstellar comets to Dyson spheres, via five-dimensional space and a sun going nova, Lunan weaves a story around the science. Lunan is such a scientist that he worries in the notes when he takes artistic licence with science, even when his change was good enough to fool Asimov.

The short stories in From the Moon to the Stars are not for everyone. However, fans of hard SF, or anyone wanting an insight into the state of SF in the early '70s, will find plenty of interest in this anthology.

It's the End of the World: But What Are We Really Afraid Of?
Adam Roberts
288 pages
Elliott & Thompson
Review by Ken MacLeod

No one would have believed in the first nine years of the second decade of the twenty-first century that so many of us would soon be slain by the humblest things that evolution in its stupidity has placed upon the earth. It is curious to recall some of the mental habits of those departed days. Pitching a survey of our imaginings of the end of the world, to be published in 2020, can't have seemed as timely at the time as it does now.

Adam Roberts' new book looks at various ways in which people have imagined the world could end. It asks why they did and do, and why these imaginings fascinate and often

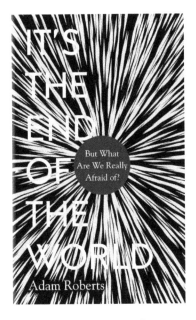

appeal to us. Along the way, Roberts gives us many sharp insights into religion, history, philosophy, and popular culture – in particular, of course, our own patch of popular culture: science fiction, which has more or less taken over from religion and even from science the burden of prophesying the End of Days.

The book opens with a summary of the Doomsday Argument: the very fact that we are alive now makes it more probable that no one will be alive in a few hundred years – because if humanity has a long future, it's much more likely that we would be alive then than now! Statistically the reasoning may be flawed, but I suspect a flaw. ('If humanity has a long future,' our descendants may say, 'we will fill the entire Galaxy, vastly outnumbering our present meagre population! How unlikely, then, to find ourselves alive now, when a mere quadrillion of us inhabit the Sagittarius Arm!')

Moving briskly on, Roberts surveys in successive chapters the ways the world might be ended, by: God or gods; zombies; plagues; machines; and aliens. He draws out the cultural and psychological meanings that each such imagined agency of destruction has conveyed. He then considers the cosmic dooms predicted by sober cosmology, and the possibility of new cosmic cycles beyond these apparent inevitabilities – the eternally springing lure of the survivalist escape pod, the hope of renewal or salvation beyond destruction. His final chapter takes us down to Earth and close to home, with the potentially world-ending catastrophe of our own making: climate change. The unexpected hopeful note here is no get-out, but a challenge: what is of our making can (if we act in time) be of our unmaking. An epilogue concludes that the root of our fascination with the end of the world is the will to make meaningful our own mortality.

This may be true at an individual level, though I find myself in my sixties less fascinated by catastrophe than I was in my teens. If there is a multiverse, my complacency is survivorship bias: I'm one of the perhaps few versions of me that didn't end in the Cuban Missile Crisis or one of several nuclear close calls in decades since. Psychological and existential issues may be the hooks by which socially available narratives latch onto our particular minds, but the existence and propagation of these narratives have to be socially explained.

Worlds have ended before: as has often been pointed out, what we think of as 'the ancient world' of Greece and Rome stood on the ruins of a world more ancient still, whose every city was burned to the ground by invaders that the Egyptians – sole survivors from that deeper antiquity, and a marvel to the Greeks – called 'the sea peoples'. For millennia it was quite forgotten. The later fates of Babylon, of Jerusalem, and of Rome still echo in the cultural memory of the West. Roberts links the original Apocalypse very clearly with its context, the catastrophic defeat of the Jewish Revolt, and its recurrent salience to other crises, from the grim year 1000 AD to Cold War II in the 1980s. The precise circumstances in which other dooms loom large and then fade from view – who now is haunted, as many seem to have been in the 1920s and 1930s, by the heat death of the universe? – seem worthy of further exploration.

These are large topics for a book of 193 pages, plus index. Within its confines Roberts has done far more than take the four horsemen out for a canter: he spurs them to a gallop and makes them break sweat. The show is well worth the price of admission, and sends us away deep in thought.

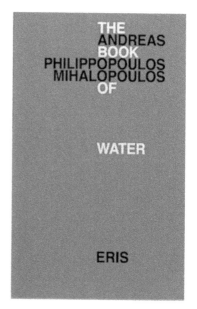

The Book of Water
Andreas Philippopoulos-Mihalopoulos
Translated by Sakis Kyratzis
Quadrant Review by Colin Kerris

This quarter, we took on a different challenge. The Book of Water *was shorter than we'd expected and only became shorter the more we read. We spent an hour walking through our understanding of what we'd read and what we could recommend to others and hit the wall, repeatedly! This is a book that we couldn't classify or even really articulate where we landed on it. Our Reviewer, Colin, summarised it and we really couldn't improve upon it!*
—*Sam*

The Book of Water is an Atlantean whodunnit, a shipwrecked puzzle box - a hauntological house of memories fashioned out of waterlogged origami. An amnesiac whodunnit set to shuffle.

This scant volume feels like a succession of people trying to tell you about a dream they just had - but in the instance of the telling, have already forgotten themselves.

It is said water has memory - this book might be that remembering. Its drifting segments unfold like parables from another dimension where reality itself functions in strange unknowable ways.

Its antediluvian psychogeography exists hazily in a dust of remembering. Never-named characters swim, float and meander through unspecified locales in imagistic curlicues, transmuting in and out of liquidity.

These ambient echoes bleed out the ghosts of psychosexual strangeness, fairy tales or morality plays. It's prose as jetsam and will likely rehydrate you.

Red Sonnet

On the day they discover life on Mars,
we'll walk over the wet sands of Walney.
The rift between us bridged only by harsh
hands held loosely; gloved, no touch, some love. We'll
talk haltingly about probes. Memories
of past explorations. I'll remember
the Viking landers in the seventies;
too young then for the Bowie songs I heard
bleeding from my brother's bedroom, not tuned
to the possibilities the singer
would bring years later. *What sex is it?* You'll
joke. I don't know. On the beach we'll linger
by the shoreline and I will drop your hand.
I can't be your man, can't be your woman.

MJ Brocklebank

Blue Sonnet

I want to streak my eye with sky-blue dust
slip on the skirts that I do§n't have to hide
rip cold dead plastic from shiny new stuff
discard it wantonly, aware, with pride
parade around with a clownish swagger
then pound out another online order
sport garish earrings that loudly clatter
when I toss back my head in chill laughter.
But that look of yours makes me pause once more
that look when I try so hard to explain
and the tears in your searing blue eyes, your
pain, your incomprehension and your pain.
So it's the Earth that I turn again to
but curb my excesses because of you.

MJ Brocklebank

MJ Brocklebank is a freelance writer and a lecturer at two Glasgow colleges.
MJ has written for television and film, as well as writing and directing the recent
short film, *You Can Run*..

t Wakes: the Madness of Whales

ph'nglui mglw'nafh Cthulhu R'lyeh wgah'nagl fhtagn
(from the Necronomicon)

something stirs in the Challenger Deep
      vast   purposive
         moving fast

             pods of whales
                 goose-beaked and sperm
                      flee   swimming up towards the light
                  their codas loud and frantic
                          filled with fear

      they breach   and scatter   careless of direction
             calling warnings out across the waves

humpbacks   rorquals   beaked   and blue
            take heed   stop feeding
       start (too late) to act as prey
                   but as they pick up speed
                     a darkness rises from the depths
                        too vast to register
                           as having any shape
                             or features

                            the Platonic Form of size

      and when   so quickly
        it attains the sunlight zone
            its form becoming visible

                        no natural
                   no Earth-born creature
                     could behold it
                     and stay sane

"That is not dead which can eternal lie,
And with strange æons, even death may die."
                (from the Necronomicon)

Peter J. King

quotations at beginning and end from H.P. Lovecraft

Children of the Night
II. Birth

months of feasting unopposed,
but then they made their fatal error:

first their strong had battened on us
draining our resilience
transformed us into cattle

        safe, domestic
           harmless
           ready to be food for those
           made weak by journeying
           so long between the stars

       maybe they had underestimated our resolve
          maybe desperation forced their hand
        maybe weakness threatened
      to bring death among them
   we may never know —
          but one night
     filled with the now familiar flights
      of feeding and of death
    one came to me...
  and I was stronger
taking from it something that I couldn't name

I spent the next week lost in fever
mind attempting to reject this alien intrusion
then I started reaching some accord with it
and finally to make a peace with it,
and form a union of sorts

my will became   a shield
                      a shell
                      a craft, a weapon
                      life support
        it hid me, held me,
            lifted, fed,
                transported me

I was the first, but not the last
                        and every night we flew above our towns
                            defending those below
                    the sleeping Earth was showered
                by their falling forms,
        the pale defeated foe.

Peter J. King

Peter J. King was born and brought up in Boston, Lincolnshire. He was active
on the London poetry scene in the 1970s, returning to poetry in 2013. His
work (including translations from German and modern Greek poetry, the latter
in collaboration with Andrea Christofidou) has since been widely published
in magazines and anthologies. His available collections are Adding Colours to
the Chameleon (Wisdom's Bottom Press) and All What Larkin (Albion Beatnik
Press).
https://wisdomsbottompress.wordpress.com/

hull breach

breathe
  first of all keep breathing
   beating heart a little
    flutter the rest is
luxury
pain   beyond
  pain is all
thought is
luxury
      now is only
         one breath eternity is only
        one breath
       one beat
only sound the scream
through me structural
integrity
compromised
  claustrophobic
   womb
    the wires
   we trained
        for this
remember the
        protocol
      they never told us
how could they
how could we
  know
    the rush
      freedom of
       oh
who knew that stars
  could sing

Sadie Maskery

Alien

Aftermath, we go on.
What then? Do we pretend
nothing was really meant,
that we knew all along,
the masks stayed in place
and the veneer never cracked?
I know you now.
I know what lies under
the neighbourly smile.
What do we do
with that knowledge,
that monsters live among us?

Sadie Maskery

Sadie Maskery lives in Scotland by the sea. Her writing in 2021 will be found in publications including those of the British Fantasy Society, Star*Line, Red Planet Magazine, Hexagon Magazine, Anamorphoseis, 5050 Lit, Dreich, and Badlung Press. She is on Twitter as @saccharinequeen where she describes herself, optimistically, as 'functioning adequately'.

A Science Fiction Ghost Story

Flash fiction competition for Shoreline of Infinity Readers

At Christmas, everyone enjoys the thrill of a ghost story. This year, we want a science fictional ghostly tale to scare the bejeesus out of us. You have 1,000 words, starting *now*.

Prizes

£50 for the winning story, plus 1-year digital subscription to *Shoreline of Infinity*. Two runners-up will each receive a 1-year digital subscription to Shoreline of Infinity.

The top three stories will be published in the December issue *Shoreline of Infinity* – all three finalists will receive a print copy of this edition.

The detail

Maximum 1,000 words, one story per submitter.

The story must not have been previously published.

Deadline for entries: midnight (UK time) **5th September 2021**.

To enter, visit the website at:

www.shorelineofinfinity.com/2021ffc

There's no entry fee, but on the submission entry form you will be asked for a certain word from this issue 23 of *Shoreline of Infinity*, so have this ready by your side.

Lightning Source UK Ltd.
Milton Keynes UK
UKHW020836010721
386451UK00003B/12

9 781838 126865